Heinemann
New Windmills

Music on the Bamboo Radio

When the Imperial Japanese Army invades Hong Kong in 1941, all Europeans are rounded up and imprisoned. But Nicholas Holford manages to escape capture. Disguised as a Chinese, he becomes involved with the Communist guerrillas. He is given the hazardous mission of 'playing music on the bamboo radio' – smuggling information and goods into prisoner-of-war camps. It is a mission full of danger: discovery will mean torture and certain death.

About the Author

Martin Booth was born in Lancashire but was brought up in Hong Kong and Kenya. His family moved to Hong Kong when he was six and he stayed there until 1964.

Martin is a keen traveller and has undertaken many adventurous journeys including walking across the Masai Mara/Serengeti in Kenya/Tanzania and rafting down the Athi River in Kenya.

As well as writing novels, Martin has written screenplays and scripted several wildlife documentaries, including David Attenborough's *Wildlife on One*. He has also made his mark in journalism as a literary critic and travel writer.

MARTIN BOOTH

MUSIC ON THE BAMBOO RADIO

Heinemann
New Windmills

Heinemann Educational Publishers
Halley Court, Jordan Hill, Oxford OX2 8EJ
A division of Reed Educational and Professional Publishing Ltd

OXFORD MELBOURNE AUCKLAND
JOHANNESBURG BLANTYRE GABORONE
IBADAN PORTSMOUTH (NH) USA CHICAGO

04 03 02 01 00
10 9 8 7 6 5 4 3 2 1

ISBN 0 435 12490 0

Cover illustration Mark Oldroyd
Cover design by The Point
Typeset by ⊼ Tek-Art, Croydon, Surrey
Printed and bound in the United Kingdom by Clays Ltd, St Ives plc

On Christmas Day, 1941, after a fortnight of bloody fighting, the British crown colony of Hong Kong surrendered to the might of the Imperial Japanese Army. Both allied military personnel and civilians were rounded up and imprisoned.

Very few succeeded in avoiding capture. Those who managed to escape took to the sea in small boats or fled overland into China.

This is the story of Nicholas Holford who, guided by fate and the love of his Chinese servants, stayed behind . . .

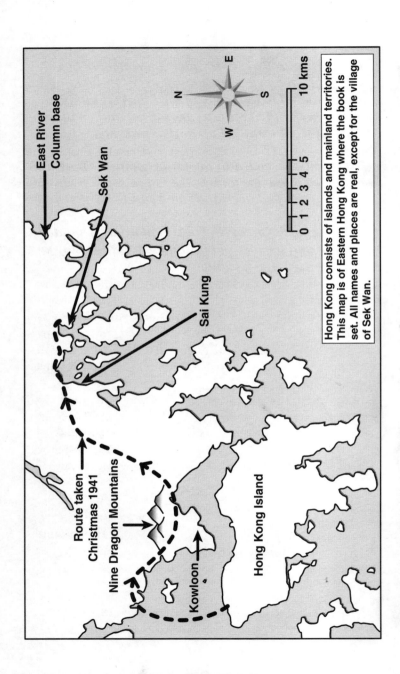

East River
Column base

Sek Wan

Sai Kung

Route taken
Christmas 1941

Nine Dragon Mountains

Kowloon

Hong Kong Island

0 1 2 3 4 5   10 kms

N
W E
S

Hong Kong consists of islands and mainland territories.
This map is of Eastern Hong Kong where the book is
set. All names and places are real, except for the village
of Sek Wan.

Part One

December 1941–February 1942

Nicholas crouched by the garden gate at the end of the gravel path. Through the hibiscus bushes and the iron railings, he could see at least a hundred metres along the street.

Nothing moved. It was uncannily quiet.

Usually the street bustled with coolies carrying loads on bamboo poles over their shoulders, amahs and other domestic servants on their way to market, passing rickshaws and handcarts laden with vegetables, squealing piglets or clucking hens. The tea-house on the corner was always busy with old men sitting at tables in front of the big brass urns, talking or playing mahjong. Their songbirds chirped in delicate cages of split cane which were suspended from the branches of the bauhinia tree overhanging the pavement.

Now, the tea-house was boarded up and the tree had been stripped of its leaves by an explosion. The square cobblestones were littered with pieces of masonry, shards of glass and the smashed woodwork of a scarlet-painted rickshaw. Its green canvas hood lay in the gutter with its umbrella-like frame twisted, reminding him of a huge, dead bat's wing. Both the wheels were buckled beyond repair. Further on, the remains of a street barber's staff leaned against a wall, the stools broken, the pavement littered with the shattered white china of the barber's bowl. They contrasted with a scatter of shattered red roof tiles.

Nicholas looked above the buildings to the steep face of Victoria Peak rising into the sky just behind them, the sheer rocks of the mountainside sheened with water. They were the only thing which seemed not to have been affected by the fighting and, he thought, maybe that was why the summit had once been called Tai Ping Shan in Cantonese: in English, the name meant Heavenly Peace Mountain.

A tabby cat appeared. Sauntering into the middle of the road, it sat and started to wash itself. Nicholas knew the animal. It lived in the grounds of the temple two streets down the hillside. He was about to call to it when it abruptly stopped licking a forepaw and glanced down an alleyway: then, in less time than it took to blink, it was gone.

Straining his ears, Nicholas could just hear a faint noise. It sounded like someone softly flapping a wet cloth on a stone.

Surely, he thought, no one could be doing their laundry. Not now, not on the morning of Christmas Day.

The noise stopped. There was a brief rustling sound. The noise began again. A voice muttered something. Nicholas tried to pick out what was being said but the voice was not much louder than a hoarse whisper.

As suddenly as the cat had vanished, a figure appeared on the pavement by the tea-house, half-hidden by the trunk of the bauhinia tree. As it moved forward, another materialized behind it. With every step the figures took came the soft slapping noise. They reached the tree, paused for a few seconds then stepped into the centre of the street.

'Japs!' Nicholas whispered to himself, sucking his breath in. His heart thumped against his ribs.

Not seventy metres from him stood two Japanese infantry soldiers. They each wore a khaki uniform, their baggy trousers gathered at the knee into webbing gaiters. From their belts hung gas masks and water bottles, ammunition pouches and grenade holders whilst on their backs they carried packs. On their heads they wore circular steel helmets held in place with cotton tape elaborately tied under their chins. In their hands were rifles with fixed bayonets.

Very cautiously, they surveyed the street, their eyes ranging over the closed doors, shuttered windows, rooftops. Satisfied they were not in any danger, they moved forward. The slapping noise was their soft rubber boots on the cobbles.

By the rickshaw, they halted. Nicholas stared at them. They seemed to be looking straight at him. One of them slowly put his rifle to his shoulder, taking aim at the hibiscus bushes, directly at Nicholas's head. His heart raced faster. He wanted to scream, jump up, shout out, 'It's all right. It's only me. Don't shoot. I'm only eleven.'

A hand clamped itself over his mouth. Another gripped his shoulder as tight as a vice, pressing him down, pulling him backwards. A mouth brushed against his ear.

'No make noise!' The words were barely audible. 'No make move quick!'

Nicholas screwed his neck round as best he could. Fingers still covered his mouth, pressing his lips painfully into his teeth. The hands belonged to a lithe and sinewy young Chinese man with close-cropped hair, small ears and a scar on one of his high cheekbones: it was Ah Kwan, the gardener.

'No talk,' Ah Kwan murmured. 'We go. Softly-softly. No sound. Slow, slow. No stand up.'

He took his hand off Nicholas's mouth and, very gradually, guided him backwards from the hibiscus bushes. Out of sight of the gate, and keeping off the path for fear of the sound of their footsteps on the loose gravel giving them away, they ran at a crouch through the gardens and up the sloping lawn to the house.

Peony Villa was a two-storey, red-brick colonial-style house with a deep veranda running all round it upon which stood rattan chairs and several tables. The

3

windows were covered by polished wooden slatted shutters. Along the edge of the veranda was a row of green glazed plant pots embossed with writhing golden dragons and containing small azalea and kumquat bushes. By the front door stood a tall palm tree, its fronds of leaves fifteen metres above the ground.

Nicholas and Ah Kwan rushed past the veranda and up the steps to the front door which opened just as they reached it. In the hallway stood Tang, the cook and head servant. With him was his wife Ah Mee. There was no need for words. The look on Ah Kwan's face told them everything they needed to know.

'No more time,' Tang declared with authority. 'No can stay. We go now.'

'We must wait,' Nicholas replied. 'When my parents get back . . .'

'No can wait,' Tang interrupted.

Taking Nicholas's arm, Ah Mee explained, 'Hong Kong no more fighting, Young Master.'

'If the fighting's ended,' Nicholas reasoned, 'the volunteer defence force will be dismissed and my father will come home. And my mother won't have any more wounded people to care for, so . . .'

'Japanese soldiers win,' Ah Mee said quietly. 'Catch all European people.'

'If we stay, catch you, too,' Tang went on, adding, 'No good. Japanese soldiers very bad people. Other servant all gone. Ah Tu, Ah Choi, Ah Peng – all gone.'

'They should have waited for my father,' Nicholas retorted.

'Master and Missy no come back here,' Ah Mee said.

From behind the big camphorwood chest next to the drawing-room door, Tang pulled four round bundles tied in blankets.

'This for you,' he declared, dropping the smallest on the lid of the chest. 'We go now.'

4

With that, he signalled to Ah Kwan who opened the front door and slipped out.

Nicholas entered the drawing room. A carriage clock ticked loudly in the still room. Beyond the settee, armchairs and a low rosewood coffee table, stood the Christmas tree. It all looked so normal, Nicholas thought, no different from any of the other Christmas Days he could remember. Glass balls hung from its silver tinsel-draped branches to which wisps of cotton wool had been stuck for snow. Beneath the tree were presents wrapped in coloured crêpe paper tied with ribbon. He knew what his gifts were because he had peeked at them one morning just after the Japanese invaded, when his father had gone off to fight with the civilian volunteers and his mother had been called away to her auxiliary nursing post. He had a model Chinese sailing junk which really sailed, a fountain pen, a book about lizards and a penknife with a tortoiseshell handle.

Looking at the clock, Nicholas felt a sharp pang of misery. It was nearly noon. His parents should have been there. They always opened their presents at midday. His mother sat on the settee with a sherry, Tang and the other servants waited by the door for their gifts and his father stood by the tree handing the packages out one by one.

On a green felt-covered card table near the clock was a chessboard. To the left of it were four white pawns, a knight and a bishop whilst to the right were two black pawns and a castle.

I was winning, Nicholas thought sadly but with a certain triumph: he rarely beat his father at chess. Yet, as he looked at the chess pieces, he realized it had been five days since the motorcycle messenger arrived and they had postponed their game. His father had grabbed his revolver, hurriedly kissing him and his mother before leaving the house. And it was, Nicholas reckoned, two days since he had seen his mother run from the house carrying her black leather nursing bag.

Ah Kwan returned. He reported the Japanese soldiers still in the street and joined by a dozen more with an officer. They were preparing for a house-to-house search.

'We go now,' Tang repeated from the doorway. 'Must go quick!' He had slung his bundle on to his back.

Nicholas had to make a decision. His mother had told him to stay near the house *no matter what*: she had made him promise that. Yet now Tang wanted him to leave immediately. His parents would not, he knew, mind him going off with the servants. He had often gone to market with Tang and had even accompanied Ah Kwan to an open-air theatre at Chinese New Year. Yet that was different: his parents had known where he was going then. Now they would not. What was more, he reasoned, his parents would be really upset if he was not there when they returned. This was no ordinary day, it was Christmas.

'Must go!' Tang insisted, beckoning urgently. 'No wait!'

'My parents . . .' Nicholas began.

'No come back!' Tang interrupted abruptly.

He was almost angry and this both shocked and dumbfounded Nicholas. Tang never lost his temper.

'No can wait,' Ah Mee said, appearing behind Tang, her bundle over her shoulder. 'Must go before Japanese come.'

'Maybe the Japs'll take me to my parents,' Nicholas suggested.

'No, he no do!' Tang exclaimed, his voice rising. 'Japanese catch you, he beat you. More hard than you father when you naughty. Maybe he kill you. You no more argue with me. Pick up!' He pointed at the bundle. 'Go now!'

Nicholas had never seen Tang like this and the sight settled his indecision. There was, he now considered, no alternative. For Tang to be so stubborn and cross there had to be good cause: neither Tang nor Ah Mee would ever deliberately make him break his word to his mother. Above all, they could be trusted for they were, to Nicholas, like family.

'Just a minute,' he said. 'I must do something first.'

'Quick!' Tang retorted brusquely.

Going to his father's writing desk, Nicholas took a sheet of paper out of the drawer and, picking up his father's silver propelling pencil, hastily scrawled upon it:

Dear Mum and Dad, I've gone with Tang and Ah Mee. I'm all right and I will come back later on. Happy Christmas. Love, Nicky.

Folding the note into an envelope, he laid it on the blotter and, almost without thinking, put the pencil in his pocket.

Nicholas, Tang and Ah Mee hastily followed Ah Kwan across the garden and, leaving it through a gate by the servants' quarters, followed a watercourse which ran through thick bushes along the hillside above the house. Over their heads towered the mountain. To their right, the tenements and steep narrow streets of Western District were spread beneath them. Beyond the buildings was the harbour, almost empty of ships, and the peninsula of Kowloon with its backdrop of hills. Eventually, they reached a shallow depression in the side of the mountain, sheltered by overhanging bushes.

'This a safe place,' Tang declared, lowering his bundle. 'We stop here.'

'What are we going to do, Tang?' Nicholas enquired.

'Night-time come, we go,' Tang answered. 'Over Kowloon-side. No good stay on Hong Kong island. Japanese can find us too easy.'

Hunched under the bushes, Nicholas looked at the three servants. He had known them all his life, for as long as he had known his parents. They were as much a part of his family as his father and mother: indeed, he had spent more time with Tang and Ah Mee than with his parents. Even before the war they had been out most of the day, his father at his office in the Hongkong & Shanghai Bank and his mother doing her charitable work or playing tennis at the Ladies' Recreation Club.

Tang squatted on the ground, fiddling with his bundle. Fifty years old, he had been cook and head servant for eighteen years and, as such, ruled the household. Ah Mee, crouched next to Nicholas, was fifteen years younger than her husband. She had joined the household when she was nineteen. At first, she had been the wash-sew-sew amah, the servant who did the laundry and repaired the clothes but, when Nicholas was born, his mother trained her into being the baby amah. From the end of his first month, she had looked after him, bathed and fed him, cuddled him and sung him to sleep, chastised him, spoiled him, taught him how to use chopsticks, taken him for walks in his wicker push-chair and, later, accompanied him to and from school. Next to Tang, Ah Kwan knelt behind a bush, scanning the city below. He had worked for the Holfords since he was Nicholas's age. A fisherman's son, his parents and elder brother had drowned in a typhoon: Nicholas's mother had found him wandering the streets of the city begging, had taken him in and trained him.

His thoughts moved to his parents. He tried to imagine where they were, what they were doing. He could picture his father in his volunteer corps army uniform and his mother in her nurse's apron but beyond that his mind was blank. Every time he conjured them up, he missed them terribly and wanted them back. Perhaps, he thought with a flash of optimism, they were actually down in the Hong Kong Club. If the fighting had stopped, he reasoned, they might have gone in for a quick gin and tonic before setting off home.

Yet, no sooner had this thought occurred to him than, without warning, a wave of intense fear spread through him. It was like nothing he had ever experienced before. A blackness of terror, it seemed to draw itself across his very soul.

'No be afraid,' Ah Mee consoled him, taking his hand. 'Tang and me look-see you safe.'

'You no worry. Be strong boy,' Tang said. 'You be strong boy, grow up strong man like your father.'

'Do you think my parents . . . ?' Nicholas began.

'Master and Missy, no problem,' Tang interrupted optimistically, giving him a smile of encouragement. 'When they come, we go see.'

'You go sleep now,' Ah Mee advised, putting her arm around Nicholas's shoulders. 'Tonight we go, no can sleep. Get rest now.'

Nicholas curled up against Ah Mee and dozed fitfully. He was woken, in the middle of the afternoon, by an aircraft flying over the city, close to the mountain, the din of its engines bouncing off the sheer rock face above. Glancing up, he saw the dull olive-grey fuselage with the red circle of the Japanese sun painted on the underside of the wing. Beneath its belly was suspended a finned bomb. It made two passes overhead then flew away over the harbour.

'That was a Zero,' Nicholas said, adding a little anxiously, 'Do you think he saw us?'

'No see us,' Tang replied with certainty. 'He go too quick. We under bush.'

As night fell, they left the depression and took a path down towards the city. Ah Kwan moved ahead, slipping from shadow to shadow, signalling them to wait or edge forward. The steep streets were eerily still. No lights shone at windows or doors. Every now and then, they met another person moving surreptitiously about in the darkness, exchanged a few muffled words and went on, ever downwards through the narrow alleyways towards the harbour.

Close to a quay, they halted and hid in a doorway whilst Ah Kwan scouted the waterfront. He had been gone less than a minute when the sound of a lorry approached, its engine grinding in low gear. The headlights swung by and, as they lit the road, Nicholas saw a dead man stretched out across the far kerb. He was a coolie, his rattan conical hat lying near his feet. The lorry went by. From its regimental insignia and number-plate, Nicholas could tell it was a British Army vehicle but, by the glow of the dashboard lights, he saw the driver was a Japanese soldier. The front wheel ran over and crushed the dead man's hat.

When it was gone, Ah Kwan appeared and, with hand signals, guided them to the quay and down some steps slippery with seaweed. At the bottom of the steps bobbed a sampan.

'Where are we going?' Nicholas asked Ah Mee as they settled themselves against the gunwales of the sampan. The water slopping about under the deck boards smelt strongly of fish.

'We go long way,' she replied. 'Over Nine Dragon Mountains. Tomorrow, walk long time.'

Ah Kwan cast the sampan off and took hold of the single stern oar, moving it to and fro with a fluid action. The bow swung round and they headed out into the harbour. The sea was utterly black with not so much as a star reflecting upon it.

*

Just as dawn was breaking, Ah Kwan steered the sampan into a beach. As soon as they were all ashore, he set it adrift. Ah Mee led Nicholas into the cover of some dense bushes whilst Tang and Ah Kwan erased their footprints from the sand with bunches of twigs. This done, Tang untied his bundle, removing several pieces of clothing which he handed to Nicholas.

'You put on,' he ordered. 'Shoes can stay but no more wear you shirt, trousers. You must look like Chinese boy.' Ah Mee produced a pair of scissors. 'Ah Mee cut you hair short all over now.'

Nicholas removed his clothes, putting on a dark blue *sam* jacket with a row of cloth buttons and wide sleeves, and a pair of baggy *fu* trousers which Tang folded for him at the waist.

'Must I have my hair cut?' he asked reluctantly.

'Must do,' Tang replied tersely. 'You have Chinese boy haircut now. No good if you wear Chinese clothes but still look like English boy. If Japanese soldier think you English, he kill you. He kill everybody.' Then he grinned and added, 'Lucky you got dark hair. If not, we must make dark colour.'

When his head was close-cropped, Ah Kwan gave Nicholas a small round hat made of varnished cane, such as coolies wore. Held in place with a cord knotted under his chin, it fitted well and completed his disguise.

Tang inspected Nicholas and announced, 'Now we go.'

Taking up their bundles, they climbed some wooden steps leading from the beach to a road. At the kerb, Tang halted.

'Today,' he told Nicholas sternly, 'you no talk. No say anything. You do what I tell you. No question. Just do. You understand?'

Nicholas thought of the dead man in the gutter and nodded solemnly. Tang smiled, touched his cheek and said, 'You no worry. Tang, Ah Mee look out good for you.'

They set off along the road. For the first half-kilometre, they might have been on a Sunday stroll. Birds twittered in the bushes, lizards rustled dry leaves as they skittered away and crickets hissed in the grass clumps. Through the trees, Nicholas could see the sea, its smooth surface lightly rippled by a dawn breeze.

Not until they rounded a corner by a clump of bamboo did Nicholas come across his first close-up sign of war. It was a black Humber saloon car, an army staff car, with its windows smashed and one of its doors torn off and lying in the road. Beside it were a dark puddle and a scattering of brass shell cases shining dully in the early, flat daylight. As they passed the vehicle, Nicholas looked away. The dark puddle was probably engine oil, but it could just as easily have been congealed blood.

It was not long before they entered the first streets in Kowloon, close to a large military barracks. Here, there was no birdsong. The tenement buildings were silent, the windows closed and doors barred. A few people scuttled here and there, walking quickly, ducking furtively into alleyways or arcades where the shops were all boarded up. Only the shop signs hanging over the roadway seemed to have much life in them. Their colourful Chinese characters contrasted with the dullness of the scene as they swung in the breeze.

For twenty minutes, they walked through the streets until they reached a wide, straight, tree-lined road called Boundary Street and set off along it. The tenements gave way to three- and four-storey apartment buildings and houses with well-tended gardens behind walls. Nicholas noticed the birds singing again and, as they passed one gateway, a chow dog wagged its curled-up tail but simultaneously growled at him.

They were about half a kilometre along this road when Ah Kwan made off at a brisk pace, breaking into a run to a road junction a hundred metres ahead. He poked his head round it then ran back towards them.

'Japanese coming,' he stammered, his breath coming in gulps.

Tang instantly turned, looking for a gate through which they could escape to hide. There was none, only a long, high garden wall.

'Stand still,' he commanded Nicholas. 'You do like we do.'

Around the corner marched five Japanese soldiers, their rifles held out, the bayonets pointing forward. They wheeled about, one of them shouting a guttural order. Behind them appeared a ragged company of about a hundred British soldiers. Their uniforms were dirty and some of them were torn or bloodstained. A number of the soldiers wore grubby bandages around their heads or arms. Alongside them moved other Japanese troops, their rifles at the ready. An officer strutted with them, his samurai sword out of its scabbard and gleaming in the sunlight.

'No look up,' Ah Mee whispered, pushing Nicholas's head down. 'Look at ground. Kowtow.'

As the column drew level with them, the three Chinese kowtowed, bowing as low as they could. Nicholas followed their example but, by twisting his head sideways, he could still see the prisoners passing by.

His thoughts went immediately to his father. Would he be a prisoner by now? Despite himself, Nicholas craned his head a little more to one side, scanning the faces of the soldiers, hoping to catch sight of his father and yet, at the same time, praying he would not see him captured and defeated.

It was now the reality of the situation dawned on him. The British were no longer the rulers of Hong Kong but the vanquished underdogs. And, like the prisoners, Nicholas too was conquered. The realization scared him yet, at the same time, it made him feel defiant. He might be beaten now, he thought, but he would not remain so. He had no idea how he would – or could – fight back: all he knew was that, if the chance arose, he would do so.

The captured troops looked exhausted, beaten, miserable. They did not speak or even march in step. Some helped their wounded comrades or carried their packs for them. Several pushed carts loaded with possessions. When one wounded soldier, a corporal with a shock of ginger hair, stumbled, the Japanese officer ran at him waving his sword. For an awful moment, Nicholas thought he was going to slash him with it but, instead, he screamed at him and struck him across the shoulders with the flat of the blade. The corporal staggered under the blow and lurched on.

As the column disappeared down the road, Tang ordered Nicholas and the others to set off again. They walked in silence. The sight of the prisoners had shocked them. When Nicholas looked at Ah Mee's face, he could see tears wet upon her cheeks whilst Tang's jaw was set in anger.

After another two kilometres, the road wound round the perimeter fence of the airport. The runway was pockmarked with shell craters and empty except for one burnt-out aircraft parked on the concrete apron, its wings warped and its tail fin riddled with bullet holes. All the terminal building windows were smashed and the air was tinged with the smell of charred rubber.

'Now we go top-side,' Tang stated, pointing to where the road climbed towards a pass in the surrounding mountains. 'No more road after we go up. Then more easy walk.'

The higher up the hillside they walked, the more tired Nicholas grew. His shins started to hurt and his bundle seemed to get heavier. He tried carrying it on his back but that only made his spine ache. By the time they reached the pass, he was panting.

'Soon we stop,' Ah Mee encouraged him. 'We come small village soon, can sit down.'

It was not long before a small hamlet came in view to the left of the road. It consisted of a line of half a dozen houses with curled tiles on their roofs and several paddyfields of dry stubble in front of the doors.

'This place call Tseng Lan Shue,' Ah Mee told Nicholas, adding, 'this name mean village with well and wall of tree all round,' in the hope that this information might interest him and take his mind off his aching legs and back.

A dog barked a threatening welcome at them as they left the road. Outside the first house, they sat on a stone bench, the dog sniffing round them cautiously. No one appeared until Tang called out in Cantonese. At the sound of his voice an old man came out of the house and, after a hurried conversation, provided them with bowls of water and strips of dried squid. Nicholas bit into his share: it was like chewing salty rubber but, somehow, it gave him new strength.

'We go long way now,' Tang told him as they prepared to leave. 'Walking on small path. A little up, not too much. More down.'

For the remainder of the afternoon, they travelled along paths which wound along the contours of the mountains, dipped into gullies, crossed streams, passed almost invisibly over grassy slopes or meandered through woodland. Every so often, a wild pig or a deer broke cover ahead of them, startling Nicholas and Ah Mee but not Tang or Ah Kwan. Neither of them faltered in their step. Whenever they came upon a village, they avoided it, keeping to the edge of the farthest fields, or just inside the cover of trees. Twice, they stopped at tumbling streams to drink and rest their feet but only for a short while. Tang was anxious to press on.

Every now and then, Nicholas glanced away to the south. There, hundreds of metres below them and over a kilometre away, he could see the sea sparkling in the bright winter sunshine. In the far distance were islands and bays and, beyond them, the open vastness of the ocean.

As dusk fell, Tang stopped and held a hurried consultation with Ah Kwan who left them to disappear into the gloom.

'Where has he gone?' Nicholas asked, leaning against a rock beside the path. Despite a cool breeze blowing up from the coast, he was sweating, his newly close-cropped hair itching under the rattan hat. His fingers were red from grasping his bundle and his arms felt numb.

'Dark soon,' Tang replied. 'Must be sure no Japanese come here.'

It was night before Ah Kwan returned and reported the way was safe. Once more, Nicholas took up his bundle. Despite the rest, he felt all the more tired as they set off.

'Have we far to go?' he asked in the hope they were near wherever their destination lay.

Ah Mee looked at Tang and said, 'Maybe one more hour. We go down now. No more walk up in hills. Now we go down to the sea.'

They descended a steep incline, crossed some fallow fields, made their way round a hamlet of houses and a temple, skirted some sampans pulled up on a beach and fishing nets hanging from trees to dry and reached a path which ran along the shore. The breeze coming off the sea was stiffer now and chilled Nicholas to the bone. Only the light of a thin new moon like a narrow sickle lit the pathway for them.

Nicholas lost track of time. It might have been a few minutes or it might have been an hour later when they arrived at a footbridge over a creek. Ah Kwan signalled for them to halt under the shadow of a spreading tree whilst he edged forward and scanned the crossing. Finally convinced all was safe, they set off to traverse the bridge. This was nothing more than several wide planks which looped from the shore to two stone pillars in the middle of the stream. As they crossed, the planks bucked and sagged under their weight. Beneath, in the bright moonlight, silver flashes indicated where a shoal of fish was twisting and turning in the current.

'No too far now,' Ah Mee whispered as they reached the far bank. 'Ten minutes . . .'

Nicholas made no response. He was too tired now to care.

At last, they mounted some stone steps, went under an archway and arrived in what Nicholas assumed was a village on the shore. He could hear waves lapping. Tang approached the first building, knocking softly on a door. After a few moments, it opened and they were ushered into a low room illuminated only by a tiny guttering oil lamp. Nicholas was shown to a hard, square chair and handed a bowl of tea which he sipped as quickly as he could, despite it being piping hot.

'You go sleep now,' Ah Mee suggested.

An old, bent lady took the bowl from him and Ah Mee, carrying his bundle, led Nicholas into another building. At the back of a room, a charcoal fire glowed under what looked like a massive stone table. Upon it was spread a padded quilt. Instead of a pillow was an oblong block of dark green lacquered papier mâché, a dragon painted on it in gold.

'This a *kang*,' Ah Mee said. 'Chinese bed. Very warm. You sleep good.'

Not even undressing, Nicholas lay down.

'Do you really think my parents are all right?' he asked drowsily as Ah Mee removed his shoes.

'No worry,' she replied in a whisper, her face pink in the light of the charcoal. She folded the quilt over him then, leaning forward, for the first time ever, she kissed him on his forehead just as his mother had.

It was snug under the quilt, the smooth stone beneath it reassuringly warm and dry. Nicholas rested his neck upon the block pillow and, within minutes, was asleep.

*

When Nicholas woke, it was mid-morning. He slid off the *kang*. The fire underneath it had gone out and the charcoal was now just a pile of grey ash. He unwrapped his bundle to find Ah Mee had packed it not with his own but with Chinese clothes and a pair of felt shoes. Yet deep inside the clothing, he found, was something which was his: it was a small silver photo frame containing a picture of Nicholas and his parents, taken when they were last on leave in England. Nicholas was sitting next to his mother in an open carriage on a miniature railway at the seaside, while his father was posing on the platform. His great-uncle Henry had taken the picture. Nicholas could see the old man's shadow on the ground, just touching his father's shoes.

Looking at it for a minute, a wave of sadness flowed through him. Yet he fought it: he had to be strong. The picture was not just a reminder of happier days but, he thought, also a test to keep him resolute. He propped it on a shelf above the *kang* then, putting on the felt shoes, went to the door and stepped outside. The sun was warm, the blue sky patched with fair weather clouds.

What Nicholas had thought in the night was a large village turned out to be only a row of two-storey buildings set against a steep wooded hillside. They were constructed of grey stone and had grey tiled roofs the ends of which curled upwards like dragons' tails. Beside each door was pasted a red prayer strip with gold characters painted upon it. The doors were not hinged but made of thick planks which fitted into a groove cut in the stone lintel. In front of the buildings was a flagstoned terrace along which ran a very low stone wall above a five-metre drop to a pathway. In the centre of the terrace grew a lychee tree, its branches spreading out over the wall. At the end, there was a narrow gatehouse over a curving passageway of smooth stone steps which descended out of sight to the path. At the other end of the terrace was a building from which a snorting noise was coming.

No one was about. He might have been alone were it not for the noise. He went towards the end building, the door of which was open, and peered in. A hen flapped its wings and ran out past him as he entered. The floor was strewn with straw and the air had an unfamiliar sweet stink to it. Looking over a wooden partition, Nicholas came face to face with a massive black pig. It raised its snout at him and snuffled like someone with a bad cold.

Nicholas was so surprised, he took a step back and bumped into an old man standing right behind him. The man's face was lined, his eyes narrowed to mere slits with age. From a mole on his chin sprouted five or six long white hairs.

'*Jiu!* Pig!' the old man exclaimed, his face cracking with a grin. 'Man pig.'

He lifted a wooden pail and poured a liquid mush into a trough. The pig started to rout about in it, sloshing and guzzling the swill. The old man pointed beyond the feeding animal to another sty.

'Lady pig,' he added.

Nicholas stood on tiptoe. He was just able to see the hairy back of another pig behind a second partition. The old man lowered the pail to the ground, took Nicholas by the hand and led him back into the sunlight. Standing in a line on the terrace were Tang, Ah Mee, the wizened old lady he had seen the night before and a girl of about his age. In the background, a black mongrel lazed in the sun. The old man let go of Nicholas's hand and joined the others.

'Ah Kwan gone. He no my family, no live here,' Tang announced rather formally before introducing the others. 'This my father and mother,' he went on, then, looking at the girl, added, 'This my brother daughter. Her name Qing-mai.'

The old man and woman bowed to Nicholas who, feeling it was the correct thing to do, bowed back. This caused everyone to break into smiles, the old woman muttering something.

'What is she saying?' Nicholas enquired.

'My mother say you a very polite boy,' Tang translated, 'got good manners, make good Chinese boy.'

'What are your parents' names?' Nicholas enquired.

After a moment's consideration, Tang replied, 'You call them Venerable Grandfather and Grandmother. Now we must work. You stay here with Qing-mai. Can help later.'

With that, the old man returned to the pigsty and the old woman disappeared into the farthest building whilst Tang and Ah Mee went out through the gatehouse. The girl giggled coyly and stepped towards Nicholas who wondered how he would be able to talk to her. His knowledge of Cantonese was, at best, very basic.

'Hello,' Nicholas said, adding as an afterthought, '*tso shan*.'

'Hello,' she replied. 'No need for you to speak Cantonese to me. I speak English. I go –' she corrected herself – 'I went to school in Kowloon. Uncle Tang say you must speak English with us. That way, my English will improve and you will not forget it.'

'Forget it?' Nicholas responded with puzzlement.

'If you live here for a long time, maybe you forget your own language. You must not. When the Japanese go, the British will return and you must be English once more.'

'I won't be here that long,' Nicholas said confidently.

'Maybe, maybe not,' Qing-mai replied, a little pensively. 'Who can say? The Japanese army is very strong, with plenty of soldiers. England is many thousands of *li* away. Now I will show you our home.'

For twenty minutes, Qing-mai led Nicholas around the buildings. They started in the pigsty, over which was a fodder store, went on to the house in which Nicholas had spent the night then passed into the main home where Tang's parents lived. It was the largest of the buildings, with a big main room, a small kitchen and a second floor made of rough-hewn planks reached by an open ladder. All the beams in the buildings were entire tree trunks blackened by years of smoke from the cooking fire or oil lamps. The next house was that in which Qing-mai lived.

'Is this all yours?' Nicholas asked, looking round at the dark rosewood furniture, a shelf of Chinese books and a framed painting on silk of sparrows sitting on fronds of bamboo.

'It is my father's home,' Qing-mai explained.

'Where is your father?'

'Like your parents,' Qing-mai said. 'My father is away because of the war.'

Nicholas thought for a moment then asked, 'Has he been captured?'

'No,' she answered with a quiet voice, 'my father is fighting.'

'Where is your mother?' Nicholas enquired.

'My mother died when I was six years,' Qing-mai replied.

The last two buildings were a storehouse containing a few agricultural tools and a small, one-roomed temple. As they approached it, the black dog he had noticed earlier rose lazily to its feet and sauntered towards Nicholas, half-heartedly wagging its tail. Nicholas, despite having always been warned by his mother not to go near what she had termed native pi-dogs in case they were rabid, gave the dog's head a stroke. Its hair was hot from the sunlight.

'What is his name?' he asked.

'The dog is called Dai Kam,' Qing-mai stated. 'This is an old name. Many dogs have it. It means Bring Gold. It is a lucky name. There,' she pointed to the tiled roof of the gatehouse where a cat lay stretched out in the sun, 'is Laan Doh Mao. Lazy cat. He sleeps all day.'

They entered the temple which contained an altar and a low stool for kneeling on. A single oil lamp flickered in front of an idol which was surrounded by a drapery of scarlet silk embroidered with a gaudy phoenix, a dragon and a bird Nicholas thought resembled a peacock. The idol itself was about a metre high, its stark white porcelain face smiling benignly from under a quaint tricorn hat with a veil. Its body was bedecked in an old-fashioned brocade gown. In front of the god stood a brass urn with a dozen sandalwood joss-sticks glowing in it, the heady blue smoke wafting up to the rafters.

'This is Tin Hau, the goddess of the sea,' Qing-mai explained, adding simply, 'She guards us.'

Leaving the temple, they went out through the gatehouse down to the path which wound through trees, parallel to the shore. For a little way, Nicholas followed Qing-mai in silence.

He went over everything that had happened since he saw the two Japanese soldiers in the street, assessing his situation. He had escaped the invaders, had crossed through occupied territory and was comparatively safe. In his mind, he pictured the prisoners of war marching along Boundary Street.

At the memory of the shabby column, a shudder of apprehension ran through him. Try as he might, however, Nicholas could not imagine his father as a scruffy, dejected prisoner. He would always be a banker in a smart suit going to his office in a black saloon car. As for his mother, he reasoned, she had not been a soldier so the Japanese might not have imprisoned her: she might well have gone back to Peony Villa, would have read his note and would not be fretting. Yet he could not help worrying, his fears nagging at him like a dull toothache in his mind.

The path turned towards the shore and went down some worn stone steps towards a small, curved beach of

22

shingle in the centre of which was a huge boulder overhung by the spreading branches of a banyan tree. A stream tumbled over the shingle into the sea. At one end of the strand a small wooded promontory jutted into the sea. A kilometre offshore was a small wooded island and, in the distance beyond that, a range of mountains sharply defined in the clear winter sunlight.

'Our village is called Sek Wan,' Qing-mai announced as she clambered up the boulder and sat on the top. 'This means Stone Bay. But my grandfather calls it Sek Lung Wan.'

'That means Stone Dragon Bay,' Nicholas replied.

Qing-mai laughed. 'You understand Cantonese well. Who taught you?'

'Ah Mee,' Nicholas admitted. 'But I'm not very good. I only know a few words. Why does he call it that?'

'The stream is called Lung Mei Kai which is Dragon Tail Stream. This is an old name, many centuries old. My grandfather says if the stream is a dragon's tail, the beach must be the dragon.'

A fishing sampan appeared around one of the promontories. It was, much to Nicholas's consternation, being oared by Tang whom he had always thought of as a cook and senior servant, never a fisherman. Turning, the craft headed inshore to run up on the shingle, its hull scraping on the smooth stones. Tang fastened a mooring line to a metal ring set in the banyan tree and beckoned to them.

'Now we help Uncle Tang,' Qing-mai announced.

Stepping up to the sampan, Nicholas saw in the bottom of the vessel a tangle of netting alive with small, twitching fish.

As Nicholas helped remove the fish from the net and drop them into two wooden pails filled with sea-water, Tang said, 'We must give you Chinese name.'

'Why?' Nicholas asked.

23

'If people come, you must look like Chinese boy, speak Cantonese. They must think you Chinese boy.' He ran his eyes over Nicholas. 'I give you Chinese name. You no more Nicholas. You Wing-ming.'

At this announcement, Qing-mai giggled. Tang grinned.

'What does it mean?' Nicholas enquired cautiously, glancing from one to the other. He would rather have chosen his own name.

'Look down,' Tang replied.

Nicholas looked down. Silver fish scales patterned his jacket, glistening in the sunlight.

'It means Always Bright,' Qing-mai declared.

*

Nicholas soon settled into life at Sek Wan and was allotted certain chores, as was everyone. His first task every day was to bring two buckets of water up from the sea and sluice out the pigsty. He chopped kindling for the fire, gutted the fish Tang caught and was taught by Venerable Grandmother how to fillet and salt them, then hang them from a pole to dry in the sun. On the hillside above the village, surrounded by trees and invisible from below, were three terraced fields irrigated by the stream. Here, Venerable Grandfather grew vegetables. Every afternoon, it was Nicholas's duty to scare away the birds from the *pak choi* cabbage seedlings.

In the evenings, when the work was done, he sat with the rest of the family in the main house. For half an hour, Tang gave Nicholas lessons in rudimentary Cantonese yet, for the best part, the family did not talk very much but busied themselves with tasks which had not been possible in the day. Tang fashioned wooden net floats or sharpened hooks, Ah Mee sewed or helped Venerable Grandmother prepare their simple meal and Venerable Grandfather squinted at a book, the oil lamp close to his face. Qing-mai spent most evenings meticulously inscribing characters into a hide-bound book with a brush pen. When Nicholas asked her what she was writing, she informed him it was a long poem about her life and would take many years to write. When he asked her to translate some of it, she refused saying it was her secret life.

Nicholas, feeling somewhat left out, found an abacus in a cupboard in his room. At first, he thought it was little more than a childish bead frame but, with Venerable Grandfather's tuition passed to him by Tang, he learnt to use it to conduct quite complex mathematical sums, his fingers flicking the polished bamboo counters to and fro with increasing speed and alacrity.

The war seemed far away, a distant memory, until one afternoon several weeks later. Nicholas was busy gutting fish on the flagstones before the houses when a shadowy figure appeared under the gateway. He was instantly alert for, since he had lived at Sek Wan, only two people had visited the village, one a wandering Buddhist monk whose bowl they had filled with food and the other a fisherman whose sampan had sprung a leak, forcing him to beach it on the shingle while he effected running repairs.

For fully half a minute, the figure stood quite motionless. It seemed to be surveying the buildings, scanning them as if it could see through the stone walls. Nicholas watched it, his mouth dry, his blood racing. At last, the figure stepped forwards into the sunlight. It was a man dressed in peasant's clothing but with a khaki-coloured floppy peaked cap on the front of which was a small red star. Over his shoulder was slung a rifle.

Despite his fear, Nicholas slowly stood up. There was something familiar about the figure which he could not quite place. Yet, as it came towards him along the terrace, he suddenly recognized the man. It was Ah Kwan.

'Hello, Young Master,' Ah Kwan greeted him hastily. 'Where Tang?'

Before Nicholas could answer, Tang appeared from the store, a scythe in one hand and a whetstone in the other.

'Japanese coming,' Ah Kwan said, ignoring any form of polite greeting. He spoke in English so Nicholas could understand. 'Maybe twenty minute. Ten man, one *gunso*.'

'What's a *gunso*?' Nicholas asked. He imagined it was a kind of weapon.

'*Gunso* Japanese small-time officer,' Ah Kwan replied tersely, adding to Tang, 'No hide Young Master. Japanese know six people live here. Must see six. Now I go.'

With that, he was gone at a run, through the archway and off along the path out of sight.

'Is Ah Kwan in the army?' Nicholas enquired.

'You no talk Ah Kwan. You no see him,' Tang retorted firmly, then his voice softened. 'Ah Kwan soldier of Communist. He fight Japanese all same Qing-mai father.'

With that, he called out to Ah Mee and his father, giving them curt instructions in Cantonese which Nicholas did not understand. This done, he looked at Nicholas and said, 'Hide you picture.'

Nicholas sped into his room, took the silver-framed photo from its shelf and stared around for a hiding place. He thrust it into the cold ashes under the *kang* but they were little more than a pile of powder soft as talcum and did not cover it.

Frantically, he searched for an alternative hiding place. He tried sliding it under the seat of the chair but the bars were too close together. He wondered if he could reach the beams above but there was no way of climbing to them. Then, by chance, he saw a thin dark line at the point where the stone base of the *kang* met the wall. Some mortar had come loose forming a crevice a centimetre wide. Nicholas poked his finger into it but could not feel the back. He pressed the frame into the gap. It slid in quite easily, stopping just as the edge of the frame disappeared into the stonework. To complete the camouflage, he sprinkled the frame with a dusting of ash.

Ten minutes later, footsteps were heard approaching along the path.

Tang gathered his family together, whispering encouragement to them. To Nicholas, he said, 'No be scared. No talk. Look down, like you very afraid. Japanese no problem for us maybe.'

When they reached the gateway, the Japanese soldiers deployed themselves ready for an ambush then burst on to the terrace, bayonets fixed, only to find four Chinese adults and two children huddled outside the door to the main house.

Without speaking, one Japanese stood guard over the little group, his rifle levelled at them whilst his comrades conducted a quick house-to-house search, rummaging in cupboards and turning the quilts over on the *kangs*. In the pigsties, they looked about for the pigs. They were not there.

Satisfied there were no other people present, the patrol joined the guard. The *gunso* stood with his arms akimbo.

'I no can talk Chinese talk. I talk English,' he announced. 'You talk English?'

'Yes,' Tang said.

'Where you pig?' the *gunso* demanded to know.

'Pig die,' Tang told him. 'Two day before.'

'Where die pig?'

Tang pointed to the sea. Nicholas, wearing his varnished cane hat and keeping his head slightly bowed, wondered where the pigs were. Only half an hour ago, they had been snorting contentedly in their sties.

'Put in sea,' Tang said, pinching his nose as if at a noxious smell. 'Die pig, no good.'

The *gunso* stepped quickly forward and slapped Tang hard across the face. Tang's head slewed sideways but he

27

did not stumble. Ah Mee squeaked with horror. Venerable Grandmother began to shiver and her husband put his hand on her arm to steady her.

'You lie me!' the *gunso* screamed. 'Where pig?'

Tang looked him straight in the face and said, 'No pig. Pig die.'

The *gunso* gave an order. The guard raised his rifle and pointed it at Ah Mee. Nicholas wanted to shout out that the pigs were not dead. They must have run off into the woods. He reasoned that, if he said that, the soldiers would run off after them and leave the family all alone. Yet he kept his head down and held his silence, casting a sideways glance at Qing-mai. She caught his eye and, to his amazement, he saw a tiny smile flit across her face. It gave him heart.

'Where pig?' the *gunso* shouted at Ah Mee.

She shook her head and said, 'No Eng Lesh.'

Stepping back, peeved at his failure, the *gunso* looked along the terrace to where Nicholas's fish were hanging on their pole to dry. Taking a soldier's rifle, he marched over to the pole, smashed it to the ground with the rifle butt and stamped on the fish, grinding them into the flagstones with his heel. The other soldiers laughed but Nicholas was enraged. And that was his mistake. He raised his head, the shadow from the brim of his hat sliding across his cheek.

The *gunso* ran at Nicholas and swung the rifle at him. He was so quick Nicholas did not even have time to flinch. The butt sent his hat spinning into the air, the chin cord tearing across his nose and bringing tears to his eyes.

'You no Chinese!' the *gunso* screamed.

Qing-mai grabbed Nicholas towards herself, yelling, 'Bruffer! Bruffer!'

The *gunso* slapped her hand away, shouting 'English! English!'

He clamped his fingers on Nicholas's jaw, ramming his face upwards, so that the sun blazed into Nicholas's eyes.

'You English!' he screamed again, his rage building further, his fingers tightening. 'You English! Where parent? Where father?'

Nicholas was terrified but his mind was quite clear. If he kept his mouth shut, he might get away with it. If he spoke English, he was done for and so, he realized, would be Tang and his family.

The *gunso* unsheathed a dagger from his belt and held it to Nicholas's throat. The steel was cold against his flesh.

'English! English!' he bellowed.

Tang, his face already swelling from the slap, stepped forwards.

'No English,' he said quietly. His calm tone seemed to mollify the *gunso* somewhat. He stopped shouting but was still clearly excited by his discovery.

'Chinese?' he muttered sarcastically, letting go of Nicholas's chin and squaring up to Tang.

'No,' Tang said slowly, his head downcast as if with shame. 'No English, no Chinese. He name Wing-ming. He my wife son. English master no good, make son with my wife.'

The *gunso* looked hard at Tang for a long moment, seeking the lie but not finding it.

'Ah, so!' he said at last. 'English no good. Very bad to Asia people. You no like English.'

'I no like English,' Tang agreed.

'Japanese good for Chinese people,' the *gunso* continued. 'You like Japanese.'

'Yes,' Tang said and he bowed. The others hastily followed suit.

The *gunso* accepted this humility, barking an order to his men. They formed up in a line, marched out of the gateway and disappeared.

For more than a minute after the footsteps were no longer audible, the little group stood quite still until, at last, Tang broke the spell of their fear.

'Japanese no problem,' he said triumphantly.

Ah Mee tended to Tang's bruised face, Venerable Grandmother and Qing-mai tidied up their belongings and Nicholas salvaged those fish which had not been trampled. As he did so, it came to Nicholas not only how very lucky he was to have been taken in by Tang and his family but also just what a risk he posed. He would have to take great care never to jeopardize them.

Venerable Grandfather disappeared. A quarter of an hour later, the pigs were back rooting in the straw of their sties. How the old man had hidden them so successfully was something Nicholas never discovered.

Part Two

September 1942

The months passed. Nicholas's life became a routine. He grew accustomed to his daily chores and his knowledge of Cantonese increased. He could understand much of what was said to him and could make simple replies, but he often mispronounced words which caused Qing-mai to giggle uncontrollably, Venerable Grandmother to cackle and Tang to frown and click his tongue with disapproval.

'If you make wrong word with strange people,' Tang warned him ominously, 'they know you not Chinese boy. You must study more hard, Wing-ming. If you make mistake, can be big trouble.'

Whenever Nicholas did make an error, he would remember it and, in the evenings, he softly repeated the correct word over and over to himself to get it right: yet, in these quiet moments with the family engrossed in their own thoughts or work, he also found his mind wandering from time to time to his parents, where they were and what they might be doing.

The balmy winter days gave way to the sweltering heat of summer. In the evenings, heat lightning flickered far out over the sea and, some days, there was torrential rain which turned Dragon Tail Stream into a swirling cataract.

Nicholas undertook new duties about the village. He had to ensure the terraced paddyfield was kept flooded so the rice seedlings, which Venerable Grandfather had nurtured from seed, could grow. This entailed periodically opening a sluice gate from the stream. He also had to maintain the loose stone wall which kept the wild pigs out of the vegetables and he had to collect the hens' eggs, which the stupid birds had taken to laying in the bamboo clump behind the houses, before the rat snakes and civet cats could find them. The task he hated most was carrying buckets of pig manure up to the fields to spread around the plants. In the hot sun, the dung smelt sickly sweet and revolting.

Most days, Tang continued to fish from the sampan, leaving early in the morning but always returning well before sunset. His catches were so good that he regularly visited a small market in a village called Sai Kung, seven kilometres away by sea, where he sold a part of his catch and some of the fish Nicholas dried.

All seemed well and unaffected by the war until one day in high summer. Tang had gone off as usual in the morning but, as the sun dipped over the mountains, he had not returned. Ah Mee was petrified with fear, imagining he had been arrested, beaten up by soldiers or murdered for his day's earnings. As night fell, they all gathered on the beach, silently watching as the sea lapped gently on the shingle. Just as the moon rose over their backs, the sampan came into view. It was moving very slowly, the oar only just rowing it. Tang was not standing at the stern, as he should have been, but slouched in it.

Nicholas, without thinking, tore off his jacket, plunged into the sea and swam out to the sampan. He clambered aboard.

'Tang! What's happened?'

Tang was barely conscious. He raised his arm but let it drop, the action too exhausting for him. Quickly, Nicholas checked Tang over for wounds but he was not injured. Taking hold of the oar, Nicholas wiggled it back and forth as he had seen Tang do. It was much heavier than he had expected.The little craft rocked crazily. Tang moaned. Yet, after a few minutes' practice, Nicholas got the hang of it and rowed the craft a zigzag course to the shore.

All that night, Tang lay groaning on his *kang*. Ah Mee mopped sweat from his brow and held his hand. In the temple, Tang's parents lit joss-sticks in front of Tin Hau, praying for her help. Qing-mai joined them for a while then came outside to sit beside Nicholas on the terrace wall.

'Tang is very sick,' Qing-mai said. 'He has a fever . . .' She paused, made a tiny whining noise then gently pinched Nicholas's arm.

'Mosquito,' Nicholas guessed. 'You mean Tang has malaria?'

'I do not know the name. A small fly bites you at night. You die. Like my mother. She had this sickness.'

In the early hours, Venerable Grandmother produced a herbal soup. It smelt, Nicholas thought, like boiled socks and he could not imagine what good it might do. This proved immaterial as Tang could not swallow it. The liquid dribbled down his chin to stain the quilt he lay upon. By dawn, he was delirious and shaking uncontrollably.

Nicholas knew exactly what was needed to cure Tang. It was quinine. His parents had kept quinine pills in the bathroom cabinet. The tonic water they drank with their gin contained it. When he was nine, he had had malaria himself. The quinine had tasted bitter and made him retch but it had saved him.

'We must get quinine,' Nicholas told Ah Mee who was exhausted by her night-long vigil.

'How we get?' Ah Mee asked forlornly. 'No shop can buy.'

'We go to Kowloon,' Nicholas replied matter-of-factly.

'Kowloon very much danger,' Ah Mee answered. 'We no can go. All people must have name chit.'

'Name chit?' Nicholas queried.

'Paper say you name, where you live.'

'You mean identity papers?'

Ah Mee shook her head in despair and muttered, 'We no got.'

'Then we must risk it,' Nicholas said, 'or Tang may die.'

After some discussion, it was decided Nicholas was right. Someone had to try to fetch quinine. Ah Mee was prepared to go but Venerable Grandmother was very worried at this prospect. She pointed out a single woman, alone in Kowloon, would be prey to Japanese soldiers who, it was rumoured, were capturing young women and shipping them off to Formosa as slaves.

'Let me go with Ah Mee,' Nicholas suggested when he was told of Venerable Grandmother's concern.

Venerable Grandfather smiled wanly and muttered something which Nicholas did not quite hear.

'What did Venerable Grandfather say?' he enquired.

'He says you are a good boy but what can you do?' Qing-mai replied.

'She would not be alone,' Nicholas said, 'and they might not bother a woman with a boy. Two are safer than one.'

For ten minutes, there was a heated discussion at the end of which Ah Mee took Nicholas's hand.

'You like son for us,' she half whispered. 'Strong in you heart. Got plenty good in you.' Then, as she had on his first night in the village, she kissed Nicholas on his brow and said, 'We go.'

There was no time to waste. They had to leave immediately, despite Ah Mee's having had no sleep. Qing-mai packed them each a bundle of dried fish and some clean clothing. Ah Mee produced a small soft leather pouch which she stuffed into her clothing. As they were about to depart, Venerable Grandmother handed Nicholas something on a length of twine.

'It's for good luck,' Qing-mai explained. 'Venerable Grandfather made it for you.'

Looking closely at it, Nicholas saw it was a tiny figure of Tin Hau, exquisitely carved from a plum stone.

'Thank you. *M'koi*,' he said, making a little bow and hanging it round his neck.

It was still early in the morning when Nicholas and Ah Mee set off along the path. It was the first time Nicholas had been this way since his arrival and then he had been too tired to notice. The path wound along the edge of a creek, crossed the rickety plank bridge and veered westwards. At every step butterflies, waking up as the sun warmed them, took to flight. Despite her tiredness, Ah Mee set a steady pace.

Just after midday, they reached Sai Kung where Ah Mee decided she had to rest for a few moments. They went towards a tea-shop outside which several tables were arrayed under a spreading tree.

No sooner had they sat down than the tea-shop owner appeared. He was a surly-looking man with a misshapen ear which curled forwards, looking as if a bizarre fungus had taken root on the side of his head. He did not speak but jutted his chin at Ah Mee as if to say, *Place your order, make it quick*. She replied too quickly for Nicholas to understand.

Her words sent the man into a rage. He shouted incomprehensibly at Ah Mee, gesticulated at Nicholas and waved his hand in the air as if to shoo them away from the table. Nicholas, keeping his face downcast, stood up to go but Ah Mee held his hand and quietly spoke again to the proprietor of the tea-house. Her words placated him. His rage died down and, instead, he leered and grunted curtly.

'What did he say?' Nicholas murmured, deeming it safe to whisper. He could see the man in the tea-house, standing at a steaming brass and copper urn.

'I say I no want tea. I just very tired. Just want sit. He say we no can sit. This no free seat. We must buy tea. He say you look long time at his ear.'

She glanced up. The man was returning with two bowls of tea, the steam rising from them catching the sunlight dappling through the tree.

'No talk now,' Ah Mee said quietly. 'You no look his ear. We no want him more angry.'

The proprietor slammed the bowls down, spilling some on to the scrubbed wood of the table. Ah Mee paid him two coins. Nicholas watched her eyes. He could tell she parted with the money with considerable reluctance. What the two bowls of tea cost might be the difference between life and death for Tang.

The tea was a delicate shade of green, piping hot and slightly flavoured with jasmine flowers. It had a reviving effect on them. When she had drained her bowl, Ah Mee went into the village temple where, very hurriedly, she lit a joss-stick in front of the altar and muttered a quick prayer whilst Nicholas stood near a huge bronze temple bell engraved with mystical beasts.

'This god name Kwan Tei,' she said as she stepped over the raised lintel of the temple door. 'He help us.'

'Where are we going?' Nicholas asked.

'We go see Dr Wu,' Ah Mee replied, then she took a firm hold of his hand. 'You listen me. If I no can go, you go.' She glanced around surreptitiously and took out a bundle of notes. 'This much money. More than two hundred dollar. You do for me?'

'Yes, of course,' Nicholas answered.

'Dr Wu house in Pak Hoi Street,' Ah Mee continued. 'Near Shanghai Street. You can find?'

'Yes,' Nicholas assured her. 'I know Shanghai Street.'

He thrust the money into his own pocket, almost stabbing his hand on his father's propelling pencil which he often carried with him, except when working in Venerable Grandfather's vegetable plot. In their rush to depart, he had forgotten to leave it behind.

At half-past one, they reached a hamlet called Ho Chung where the road to Kowloon began. Parked under the shade of a tree was a very dilapidated Ford lorry, its exhaust belching smoke. Around the tailgate mingled a crowd.

'Kwan Tei listen me,' Ah Mee whispered. 'We ride now.'

Not wanting to spend precious money, Ah Mee haggled with the driver, finally making him accept a fare of four dried fish. As the engine revved, they climbed on to the back with all the other people.

*

The lorry halted in a back street, the passengers quickly getting off to melt away into the surrounding alleys and doorways. No one said goodbye to his fellow travellers. There was no time. Everyone had to be out of sight before a Japanese patrol spotted them. The lorry moved off the moment the last passenger's foot touched the ground.

Nicholas and Ah Mee hurried in silence down a passage between two closed shops and arrived at a main street. On either side, the pavements ran beneath arcades. Usually, they would be thronged with shoppers but there was hardly a soul about. The shops were closed and there was not a single hawker selling vegetables or rice bowls, offering to sharpen knives or write letters for illiterate coolies. Curious, and seeing no one anywhere near them, Nicholas decided to risk a question.

'Where is everyone?' he whispered.

Ah Mee did not look at him. She kept her eyes fastened on the street.

'All people stay home,' she said quietly. 'Only come out do business.'

'But the shops are all shut. Why isn't even a single one open?'

'Shop no got too much to sell,' Ah Mee replied. 'Hong Kong very poor place now. No business, no money.'

'People still have to go to the shops,' Nicholas reasoned. 'They still have to buy food.'

'Hong Kong no too much food now,' Ah Mee said bluntly.

They set off walking along an arcade, Ah Mee holding Nicholas's hand. Her grip was so tight he had to wriggle his fingers to keep the blood flowing. People passed them, their heads bowed. A few carried small parcels but no one carried the kind of thing Nicholas used to see. Before the war, he could have stood on a street corner for ten minutes and seen passers-by or coolies carrying live hens trussed in bamboo twine, twitching fish or bloated frogs in baskets, bags of rice or dried mushrooms, whole roast suckling pigs with their skin the colour of polished camphor wood, boxes of tea, sacks of flour or Taikoo sugar, bunches of tiger lilies, bundles of vegetables or dried fish. Never, he thought, would he have guessed that one day it would be his daily chore to dry such fish.

Turning a corner, they were suddenly confronted by a Japanese patrol blocking the arcaded pavement. They were searching a man whom they had pinioned against the wall, his face pressed into the stone, a bayonet hard against his spine.

'No look, no look!' Ah Mee hissed, her step faltering. 'No talk, no stop!'

They walked on, coming closer and closer to the patrol, not daring to change direction for fear of arousing suspicion. The Japanese officer in charge leafed through the contents of his prisoner's wallet, flicking bits of paper and a photograph into the air, letting them flutter to the ground. With each piece of paper, he became more irate.

Ah Mee's fingers tightened even further. Nicholas felt himself break into a sweat. He realized the Japanese were looking for the man's identity papers – and he and Ah Mee had none.

They drew nearer still. The officer started to tear up some currency notes, letting the shredded money drift down to join the photograph. The soldiers were having a bit of cruel fun with their unfortunate victim, prodding him with their rifle butts and drawing their fingers around his throat in a hideous mockery of killing him.

It seemed as if they were too busy at their savage sport to be bothered with a woman and her son but, just as Nicholas and Ah Mee passed the soldiers, stepping into the gutter to avoid them, one turned, reached out and grabbed Ah Mee by the shoulder, spinning her half round. Nicholas, still firmly held by her, nearly lost his balance.

The soldier put his hand round Ah Mee's neck, pulling her face to within centimetres of his own. Nicholas was terrified. His head was swimming with panic. Against Ah Mee's orders, he looked up. The soldier was a good-looking young man with a soft forage cap on his head, his rifle slung over his shoulder. His leather belt and ammunition pouches shone with polish, the black handle of his bayonet hanging in its scabbard was as glossy as jet. Seeing the blade still in its sheath somehow calmed Nicholas. If the soldier was going to kill Ah Mee, he would have taken it out.

With a quick movement, like a snake striking a mouse, the soldier tugged Ah Mee's head to his own and kissed her hard on the mouth. Several of his comrades laughed uproariously. Then he let her go. She staggered back, Nicholas lurching with her. The soldier started to step towards them but the officer barked an order and he turned his attention back to their prisoner.

As they hurried on, Nicholas glanced back. The man was lying on the ground and the soldier who had kissed Ah Mee was standing over him, wiping his bayonet on the prone figure's trouser leg.

In the next street, Ah Mee halted in an alleyway and let go of Nicholas's hand. She was quite silent but tears ran down her face, dripping off her chin like drops of rain. Nicholas reached up and wiped them away with his sleeve.

'It's all right, Ah Mee,' he consoled her. 'We're safe now.'

'Japanese man bad man,' she muttered through clenched teeth. She stepped a little way down the alley and found a standpipe with a tap. Turning the brass knob, a trickle ran out. For at least a minute, Ah Mee splashed water into her face, scrubbing at her lips with her wet fingers.

At last, they reached Pak Hoi Street and found the door of the building in which the doctor lived. Beside it, a tarnished brass plate screwed to the wall announced *Dr Wu Hsiang-lo – General Practitioner, Specialist in Tropical Medicine and Diseases of Ladies* in both English and Chinese. Ah Mee opened the door and they ascended a dark staircase. The steps creaked and the air smelt faintly of carbolic soap and methylated spirits.

The doctor's surgery was nothing more than a room in the centre of which stood a cracked leather couch. Near it was a desk with a black telephone and two chairs. No sooner had they entered than another door opened and the doctor appeared. He was an elderly man dressed in a long flowing *cheong sam*, the hem brushing against his cotton slippers. Upon the end of his nose was a pair of gold-framed spectacles. The nail on his left-hand little finger was at least four centimetres long and looked like a talon. This, Nicholas knew, was the sign of a learned man who never did manual labour.

For a moment, the doctor studied them both then, looking straight at Nicholas, he said in English, 'Hello. What is your name?'

Nicholas was so amazed, his mouth nearly fell open but he caught it just in time. How did the doctor know he was English! He had his varnished cane hat on and was wearing Chinese clothes.

'Come now,' the doctor urged him. 'You speak English.'

'Wing-ming,' Nicholas said at last. He reasoned he might get away with that. After all, he could be a Chinese who spoke English or, as Tang had told the Japanese *gunso*, he could be half-Chinese.

'No, your English name,' Dr Wu asked with a kindly voice, leaning forward and removing the hat. 'You are English.'

So flabbergasted was Nicholas, he replied, 'Nicholas.'

Dr Wu laughed and continued, 'You wonder how I know? It is because I am a doctor. I study people. I can tell what a person is, or what a person is not.'

He moved behind his desk and sat down. Nicholas looked at Ah Mee. Her face was stiff with anxiety.

'Your secret is safe with me,' Dr Wu said. Ah Mee's face relaxed somewhat. 'Only together can we survive this bad time. Yet do not trust everyone. There are people who work for the enemy. They kill their fellow countrymen and hoard food to sell at high prices. They are evil men.' He paused for a moment then, brightening, went on, 'Now, what do you want of me?'

'We need quinine,' Nicholas answered. 'Ah Mee's husband is sick with malaria.'

Dr Wu pursed his lips.

'All medicines are very scarce in Hong Kong now. The Japanese keep them in a store and do not release them. Quinine is very rare indeed.'

'Can you get some for us?' Nicholas asked.

'Perhaps, a little, but it is very expensive.'

From his pocket, Nicholas tugged the roll of notes Ah Mee had given him and passed it to Dr Wu who unfolded it.

'Money is no good,' Dr Wu said. 'No one wants money. All money is Japanese. It is good for buying in the market but not for medicine.'

At this, Ah Mee opened the small leather pouch, removing two jade rings and a jade figure of Kwan Yin, the goddess of mercy. She placed these carefully on the desk. Dr Wu picked up the goddess.

'A fine piece,' he remarked, turning it over lovingly in his hands and putting it back on the desk, 'but no one will buy it. Jade is no good for trade now. People only want gold or silver.'

Ah Mee felt inside the pouch again and took out two silver Mexican dollars and a very small gold coin with a dragon curling on one side of it. Dr Wu picked up the gold coin and weighed it in his hand.

'Not very heavy,' he commented. 'Maybe not enough.'

'I got no more,' Ah Mee said, her voice flat with worry and disappointment.

'I have this,' Nicholas said. With a stab of sadness, he slowly placed the propelling pencil beside the coins.

'A very good pencil,' the doctor declared, holding it in his right hand and scribbling a few characters on a scrap of paper next to the telephone. 'Where did you get it?'

'It is my father's,' Nicholas said, adding, 'It is silver. I think.'

Dr Wu smiled benevolently and stood up.

'You show much kindness,' he said, handing Nicholas the pencil back, 'and I should like such a fine pencil but you must keep this, for it is of your family.' He scooped up the three coins with his hand. 'I will go now. You stay here. I will come back in thirty minutes.'

With that, Dr Wu left the room, his feet creaking on the stairs. The door to the street closed and all was silent. Ah Mee collected up the three pieces of jade and returned them to the pouch.

Nicholas looked around the room. To pass the time, he read the framed medical certificates hanging on the wall and was astonished to discover that one of them was from the University of London where, according to the cursive lettering printed on the parchment, the doctor had obtained his degree in medicine. This gave Nicholas a surge of confidence. Dr Wu, he considered, was a man to be trusted. Finally, his eyes alighted on a poster of a naked human body with hundreds of lines drawn out from it, labelled with Chinese characters.

'Ah Mee,' he whispered, 'what is that picture for?'

'This a picture for acupuncture,' Ah Mee explained. 'All over you body are places where *chi* is strong.'

'What's *chi*?'

'*Chi* is life,' Ah Mee said enigmatically. 'If you no *chi*, you die.'

'And what's acupuncture?' Nicholas went on.

'Doctor push small needle in, turn very slow, make you better.'

Nicholas felt the skin on his spine contract. If there was one thing he hated it was going to the doctor twice a year for a cholera injection. Just the thought of the needle made little electric sparks jump up his back.

'And what's that naked lady for?' he asked, pointing at an ivory carving of a reclining nude woman. It was at least forty centimetres long.

For the first time that day, Ah Mee smiled.

'In old time, when Chinese lady go to the doctor she not want the doctor touch her. She no take her clothes off. Even now, some lady no like take clothes off. But if no take off clothes, how to tell doctor where you sick? So, if no take off clothes then lady point to this to show where she sick. Doctor then can know and make her better.'

Nicholas was still pondering on this when, ten minutes later, Dr Wu returned, handing a tiny envelope to Ah Mee.

*

It was four o'clock when they left Dr Wu's surgery to set off on their return journey. Nicholas reckoned walking all the way would take them the best part of nine hours – if they did not stop. He was doubtful, as they turned the end of Pak Hoi Street, if Ah Mee could make it. She was already exhausted and the sun, shining mercilessly from a clear sky, made the pavement hot and the air sweltering. Twice in the first mile, Ah Mee's footsteps hesitated: yet she would not be beaten and somehow found a new reserve of strength and resolve within her.

After walking for about an hour, they came upon a labour detail of British prisoners of war digging a ditch in the dusty, barren soil of the roadside. Japanese guards sauntered about, occasionally shouting orders. Working with the prisoners were a number of coolies. Every man was stripped to the waist, his skin plastered and his hair caked with dust.

From under his hat, Nicholas surveyed the prisoners as he passed. They were the first Europeans he had seen for nine months and he wondered if, perhaps, he might recognize one of them or even, he dared to hope for a fleeting moment, see his father.

They were in poor shape, lean and hungry-looking, their hair cropped short like a convict's, their uniform shorts ill-fitting and ragged in places. Some had open sores on their cheeks and chins. Where they were not tanned, their skin had a pallor to it.

The guards paid Ah Mee and Nicholas not the slightest attention and would have continued to ignore them had not Ah Mee stumbled and dropped her bundle. Two guards, seeing her totter, interpreted her action as a possible ploy to communicate with the prisoners. They ran down the line of the ditch, shouting in high-pitched voices, unslinging their rifles from their shoulders.

Nicholas tried to help Ah Mee to her feet. She was so tired she could not, for a moment, focus her thoughts.

'Get up!' he hissed. 'Get up, Ah Mee. Japanese coming.'

'No talk,' Ah Mee murmured, hardly coherent.

'Get up! Please, get up!'

Yet Ah Mee remained on her knees on the dusty road, her bundle on the ground before her. The Japanese were upon them. All the prisoners and coolies stopped work to watch the spectacle. The first guard kicked Ah Mee's bundle down the road and started screaming at Nicholas. The second stood with his rifle aimed at Nicholas's head.

'No need for that, you grubby little yellow mucker!' shouted one of the prisoners.

Nicholas scrabbled on the dirt, trying to raise Ah Mee.

'*Hei! Hei!*' he whispered. 'Up! Up!'

Ah Mee just groaned. The Japanese who was aiming his rifle at Nicholas cocked his weapon. At the metallic click, the hairs rose on the nape of Nicholas's neck. His scalp started to itch with sweat. He was on the verge of sheer panic yet his wits told him he had to do something, say something. At the same instant, he guessed the Japanese would not speak Cantonese so, on the spur of the moment, he made up nonsense.

'*Me ching nah tuk mew go shan!*' he shouted, trying his best to imitate a Chinese accent. '*Noh pau tiu mey sing faa cho,*' he went on. '*See lan cheung pay how sik ho.*'

The Japanese stared at him. Nicholas, sensing the advantage was his, stood up, checked that the cord of his hat was tight then bowed from the waist, as low as he could without falling forwards. At this, the two Japanese roared with mirth and the guards up and down the line joined in. The prisoners were silent: they knew Japanese laughter could lead to a Japanese beating in the flick of a wrist.

Nicholas remained bowing in the hope the Japanese would move away. They did not. He could see their shadows on the ground in front of him. Suddenly, they were joined by another shadow. A hand clamped on to his shoulder and he started to shiver with fear. Slowly, he straightened himself.

Beside Nicholas stood one of the coolies from the work detail. His face was crusted with sweat and dust yet, through it, Nicholas could see a scar under one eye.

The coolie was Ah Kwan.

For a moment, Nicholas stared at him. Ah Kwan stared back, his intense look begging Nicholas not to react, not to speak, not to recognize him.

One of the Japanese shouted something and turned away, his comrade following him. The prisoners recommenced their digging. Ah Kwan helped Ah Mee up and led her and Nicholas to a barrow containing a bucket of water. He ladled some into a bowl and handed it to Ah Mee. She slurped it thirstily. All the time, he did not look at them but spoke in a barely audible undertone.

'Young Master no see me,' Ah Kwan muttered.

'I no see you,' Nicholas agreed quietly.

'You drink,' he said, refilling the bowl for Nicholas. 'Then you go. No run.'

'Are you a prisoner?' Nicholas whispered furtively as Ah Kwan handed him the bowl.

'Not prisoner. No ask. No talk now,' Ah Kwan replied darkly. 'Drink. Go.'

Nicholas drained the bowl. Ah Kwan returned to the work detail, taking up a pickaxe and swinging it into the earth. Collecting her bundle, Ah Mee and Nicholas set off once more, not daring even to glance back. For the next mile, Nicholas's legs felt weak but not because his muscles were tiring. It was from the realization of how close he had come to capture.

When they reached the point where the road started to ascend towards the mountain pass, they did not stop to gather their strength but started directly upwards. Ah Mee walked like an automaton, her every step almost mechanical. Nicholas walked by her side, carrying her bundle. They did not speak: to talk was to waste energy.

The last time Nicholas had come this way, on their flight to Sek Wan, his shins had ached walking up this hill. Now, he had not even a quick stab of pain and he realized how much stronger he was after his months of working in the village.

At last, they reached the top and headed towards the village where the old man had given Nicholas the strip of dried squid. As before, a dog barked at them as they made their way along the path, warning the villagers who were working in the fields. The sun was near the horizon by now, the air was cooler and the eastern sky was dotted with cumulus clouds in front of a rising moon only a few days off full.

'Not far now, Ah Mee,' Nicholas said to encourage her as they approached the houses, 'then we go downhill for a long way.'

In response, Ah Mee sat down heavily on the stone bench by the first house.

'I no can go,' she sobbed. 'I hurt too much. Too tired.'

'We must, Ah Mee,' Nicholas pleaded. 'Please stand up.'

Yet Ah Mee remained on the bench, her head in her hands, weeping uncontrollably.

Nicholas knew there was nothing for it. Tang's life depended on him now.

'Give me the quinine,' he said.

Ah Mee looked blankly up at him.

'You'll be safe here,' Nicholas declared. 'The people will look after you while you sleep. Now,' he repeated, 'give me the quinine.'

Unquestioning, Ah Mee reached for her pouch and removed the little envelope. Nicholas took it and, without a word, set off at a jog past the houses and on to the path. He very quickly established a rhythm, humming under his breath in time to his steps. The sun set and the short twilight soon gave way to a moonlit night. The path was clearly visible and Nicholas kept going, stopping only twice to drink from a stream. Barking deer called in the trees and wild boar snuffled in the undergrowth. Every now and then, an owl hooted. Once it was dark, he removed his hat, letting it hang down his back by the cord. He met no one. Even the little villages through which he passed were shut up tight. He could hear people in the houses but he saw not a living soul.

Twice, Nicholas took the wrong path and had to double back on himself but finally, well after midnight, he arrived at Sek Wan, his legs numb from the impact of running, his head pounding and his lungs feeling as if they were lined with sand. Qing-mai gave him a bowl of fish broth as Venerable Grandmother administered Tang his first dose of quinine.

By the next morning, Tang's fever was broken. Ah Mee returned later in the day, her feet sore and her clothes filthy. The first thing she did, even before going in to see her husband, was to hug Nicholas so closely he could hardly breathe.

Part Three

April and May 1943

Late one spring afternoon, Nicholas was sitting on the wall of the terrace with Qing-mai who was busy writing her life poem. His silver pencil in his hand, he was drawing the view in a sewn notebook with coarse bamboo board covers. He was struggling to get the perspective right when a sampan interrupted his vista. It was Tang, returning earlier than usual from the market in Sai Kung, bearing a small package wrapped in red paper. Once landed, he took the package straight into the temple, placing it on a table next to the altar. Then, without speaking to anyone, he went out through the gatehouse and disappeared along the path to the promontory.

'Where is Tang going?' Nicholas asked.

'To find a flower,' Qing-mai replied, not looking up.

'What flower?' he rejoined.

'The flower which kills the bite of a *kit gee*,' she said.

Nicholas was puzzled. He was now quite fluent in Cantonese but his vocabulary was still somewhat lacking and this was something he had never heard before.

'Give me your pencil,' Qing-mai demanded and she drew a rough picture in Nicholas's book.

'That's a scorpion,' Nicholas said. 'There aren't any flowers which can cure a scorpion sting.'

'There is,' Qing-mai retorted. 'The Emperor Kao Tsung gave it to his followers and told them to wear it in their hats for safety. On the third day of the third moon. Today is the second day.'

Tang reappeared on the path below them, carrying two branches of pussy willow. He came up to the terrace and broke off two twigs, the pollen on the catkins drifting like gold dust in the warm sunlight.

'Tomorrow is Ching Ming,' he told Nicholas. 'Now you are our son you must come with us.'

'Where do we go?'

'To visit the golden pagodas,' Qing-mai answered enigmatically. 'And you must carry this flower or, when you die, you may be reborn as a dog.'

Nicholas thought that was a load of tosh but he kept his counsel.

That evening, their meal was cold and no fire was lit in the stove despite a chilly wind coming off the sea. When Nicholas queried this, he was told it was not good to light a fire the night before Ching Ming.

'What is Ching Ming?' Nicholas enquired as he tried to swallow a piece of cold fish.

'Ching Ming is the Festival of Spring,' Qing-mai told him. 'It is when the world wakes up after the cold months. *Ching* means clear and *ming* is the same as your name: bright.'

'And where,' Nicholas went on, curiosity having burned in him since the afternoon, 'are the golden pagodas? Are they far away?'

Certainly, he knew of no golden pagodas within several kilometres of the village for he had covered the ground fairly well gathering firewood. Furthermore, he had not seen any on his journey to the village or when fetching the quinine.

'No long way,' Tang said.

'Do we go by sampan?' Nicholas asked.

'No,' Tang replied, 'we walk.'

The next morning, they all set off towards the promontory. Everyone except Tang and Venerable Grandfather wore a sprig of pussy willow.

Tang led the way, carrying the red package in both hands. Behind him went his parents, bringing between them a larger parcel wrapped in more red paper. Ah Mee bore a basket behind them. The little procession ended with Qing-mai who held a bamboo broom and, last of all, Nicholas.

The wind sang mournfully in the branches of the pines. The path narrowed the further out they went on the promontory; finally, it all but disappeared near an outcrop of huge boulders. Tang turned towards these, Venerable Grandfather cutting the path wider with a long-bladed knife. At last, rounding the outcrop, they came to a gentle hillside covered in low scrub. Halfway down was a horseshoe-shaped platform of beaten earth at the rear of which was a small stone slab set vertically into the ground beneath a smooth boulder. Nearby, half-hidden in the scrub, was a row of six brown-glazed earthenware urns the size of small barrels.

'Those are *kam taap* – the golden pagodas,' Qing-mai said, 'and this flat place is our family grave. Behind there,' she pointed to the slab, 'is where Venerable Grandfather's father lives.'

'Now,' Tang announced to Nicholas, putting his parcel down, 'we do *sau mu cha liu*. This mean clean grave and put on flowers.'

Everyone set to tidying up the place. Tang cut back the scrub and grass to a distance of several metres, Nicholas assisting him to build two heaps of cuttings. Whilst Qing-mai swept the platform clear of twigs and leaves, Venerable Grandfather knelt on the ground and painstakingly painted in some characters carved on the slab with vermilion ink. Ah Mee and Venerable Grandmother opened up the parcels and basket to produce a bottle of wine, dried fish, some joss-sticks, two oranges and, to Nicholas's amazement, a glazed roast duck.

When the area was cleared, Tang placed three little bowls in front of the slab and filled them with wine. The dried fish and the duck, its crisp skin glistening like varnished wood, were put beside them. This done, he lit three joss-sticks and stuck them in the earth. Everyone very solemnly bowed. Nicholas, out of politeness, copied them.

'Now we must go to visit the golden pagodas,' Qing-mai announced.

The little party left the grave and approached the urns. Venerable Grandfather removed the six lids. Nicholas peeked into the first urn. Inside was a complete human skeleton, the bones disjointed and arranged so the skull balanced on top.

'These my ancestors,' Tang said reverently. 'This pagoda, my aunt,' he pointed from one urn to the next, 'this one my father uncle. This his brother. He die more than fifty years before.'

After more bowing, they all returned to the grave where Ah Mee sliced up the duck.

'This duck is for our ancestors in heaven,' Qing-mai said. 'They finished eating now.'

'How can they eat it?' Nicholas enquired. It made no sense to him: dead people could not eat roast duck.

'They eat meat ghost,' Ah Mee explained, handing Nicholas a piece. 'Now we eat.' She smiled. 'Now we have food with our family.'

Nicholas bit into it. The flesh was dry but the skin was crisp, succulent and flavoured with herbs. With the meal consumed, Nicholas assumed they would return to the village but there was still one part of the proceedings left undone.

'Wing-ming,' Tang said, beckoning to Nicholas and leading him to the smaller pile of cut scrub, 'now we burn *yuen po*. You help me. Venerable Grandfather too old.' He handed Nicholas one of two small packets. 'I burn other wood, put on *yuen po*. When I do this, you open packet, also do like me. Be quick! You must burn you *yuen po* for devils. He come you fire, take you *yuen po*, no see my *yuen po* go to my ancestors in heaven.'

With that, Tang bent down and kindled the pile with a match and some dried moss before walking quickly to the other pile which he also ignited. The others watched from the grave platform. Nicholas understood his instructions. He was to burn the contents of the packet when Tang did likewise on the other bonfire. What worried him was the mention of devils coming to his bonfire. Did they, he wondered, materialize from the sky or from the ground? And would they harm him?

The smoke drifted up the hill on the breeze. Flames crackled in the dry twigs. Tang split open his packet and Nicholas followed suit. Inside was a thick wodge of banknotes. Nicholas glanced at Tang. He was putting his on the fire. Although he was confused, Nicholas obeyed Tang's order. The paper curled and burned. To his relief, no devils appeared. It was not until he reached the last banknote that he saw what was printed on it: it read, in English, *Hell Bank Note 1,000,000 yuan*. He turned it over. On the reverse was printed the portrait of a fierce-looking warrior god.

'It's toy money,' Nicholas said.

'Not toy money,' Qing-mai replied, a roll of notes in her hand. '*Yuen po*. Spirit money. When you burn, it go to heaven.' She cast her wad on to Tang's fire.

'You mean like burning a letter to Santa Claus?' Nicholas asked but Qing-mai did not understand and just smiled.

After more spirit money was placed on top of the golden pagodas and weighted down with stones, the party left the hillside and returned to the village. Making his way back through the whispering pines, Nicholas thought over the simple ceremony. This had been, he considered, one of the strangest days of his life. But it was not yet over. Before the moon rose, his life was to take a dramatic and terrible turn.

*

As night fell, soft footsteps heralded the unannounced arrival of Ah Kwan and a stranger. He was a tall, angular Chinese with a prominent Adam's apple. He was dressed in the clothes of a peasant farmer but, under his coat, he wore a bandoleer of ammunition across his chest. He carried a sub-machine-gun which he laid against the wall of the temple beside Ah Kwan's rifle, the oiled metal gleaming in the last hint of daylight.

In silence, he and Ah Kwan shook hands with Tang. Venerable Grandfather kowtowed to the stranger who put his hand on the old man's arm, raising him up and bidding him not to bow. Tang called to Nicholas and stood him in front of the stranger, speaking so quickly to the man Nicholas only recognized his English name followed by Wing-ming.

'This man is a very brave man,' Tang explained at length. 'He is a general in his army. They call him General Tai Lo Fu. It mean Big Tiger.'

'Is he really a general?' Nicholas asked somewhat sceptically.

He had seen a real general at a parade in Murray Barracks when Hong Kong celebrated Empire Day and that one had looked nothing like the man standing before him. The real general had worn a pristine uniform, a scarlet band around his peaked cap and highly polished insignia and buttons.

'No general like in English army,' Tang said. 'But all same leader, top number-one man.'

'What is his real name?' Nicholas asked.

'We no say his real name,' Ah Kwan said. 'Too much danger for him if people know. You call him Tai Lo Fu.'

Nicholas made a little bow, offered his hand and said, '*Nei ho ma*, Ah Tai Lo Fu.'

At this the man's face, which had been solemn and serious, broke into a wide grin which showed one of his teeth capped with gold.

'*Ho!*' he exclaimed and he ruffled Nicholas's hair.

With that they entered the main house where Venerable Grandmother was busying herself at the stove. Within a few minutes, bowls of tea and small buns were served to the visitors who spoke at length with Tang and Venerable Grandfather, their voices subdued. Several times, Ah Kwan left the house to step on to the terrace and survey the path and bay, listening intently to the sounds of night insects. Silent insects could signal danger.

As their conversation progressed, Nicholas began to feel uneasy because, every so often, they looked at him and, though he was unable to keep up with their subdued and rapid speaking, he sensed they were talking about him. What was worse, on more than one occasion, Venerable Grandfather and Qing-mai also glanced in his direction whilst Ah Mee seemed deliberately not to be looking at him. At last, Tai Lo Fu ate the sole remaining bun and Ah Kwan turned to Nicholas.

'Wing-ming,' he said in Cantonese, beckoning to him, 'come here.'

Nicholas joined the men at the table, feeling not a little flattered to be invited to share in their conversation.

'Tang tells me you can speak Cantonese now.'

'He has been teaching me,' Nicholas replied in Cantonese.

Tai Lo Fu smiled as Nicholas spoke but made no comment.

'I am going to tell you a great secret,' Ah Kwan announced, keeping his voice low. 'You must not tell anybody. If you do, you may die. You understand?'

Nicholas nodded. Any sense of flattery evaporated. He became aware now there might be more to the invitation than met the eye.

'Tai Lo Fu and I fight the Japanese,' Ah Kwan continued. 'Our army is called the East River Column. But we are not soldiers like your father. We have no uniform, we do not go marching in parades. We live over the mountains. Nobody knows where. At night, under cover of darkness, we go to Hong Kong or into Kowloon and fight the Japanese. Not big battles like your father fought. We have no big guns, no airplanes. We have only small guns like these.' He glanced in the direction of his rifle and the sub-machine-gun where they now stood ready by the door. 'And we have knives. We do not kill the Japanese with a big noise. We do it,' he reverted to English for a few words, 'softly-softly, no sound.'

He paused to drain the tea in his bowl. Venerable Grandmother refilled it. Nicholas remembered the last time Ah Kwan had muttered those words to him. It was by a hibiscus bush near a gate on a path on a morning that seemed a long, long time ago.

'The English army in China helps us,' Ah Kwan went on, 'sends us guns. Tai Lo Fu's gun is made in England. It is called a Sten gun. It's a very good gun. It can shoot bullets very quickly. Now, the English have sent us something new.'

At this point, Tai Lo Fu interrupted. Ah Kwan replied curtly then returned his attention to Nicholas.

'Tai Lo Fu says I should not tell you too much. He says you are only a small boy but I have told him you are a good boy, a strong boy, an English boy – not like the Japanese.'

'No,' Nicholas confirmed, looking directly at Tai Lo Fu and speaking in Cantonese. 'I am not like the Japanese.'

Tai Lo Fu did not speak but reached out and shook Nicholas's hand as if sealing a deal between them.

'So,' Ah Kwan carried on, 'the English army has sent us a box but inside everything is in English writing. We cannot read it. We want you to come and help us.'

It took Nicholas a moment to appreciate what he was being asked to do. Ah Kwan wanted him to accompany him and Tai Lo Fu to their hide-out to translate something from English into Cantonese. The very thought of going off with these two men sent a frisson of excitement through him.

'Will you come?' Ah Kwan enquired.

Nicholas wanted to go. It would be an adventure and would probably last a few days. He could, he thought, do with a brief respite from swilling out the sties and spreading pig dung on the fields: and yet he did not want to go against the wishes of Tang and Ah Mee.

'Do you think I should go?' he asked them in English.

Ah Mee made no reply but Tang answered, 'Much danger for you maybe. I no can tell you. This for you to say.'

'Then,' Nicholas decided firmly, 'I will go and look at the box.'

Within a quarter of an hour, Nicholas was walking over the bridge at the creek. As he kept pace between Ah Kwan and Tai Lo Fu, the planks bounced under their tread.

The moon was not due to rise until the early hours, yet the night was not entirely dark. Once his eyes grew accustomed to it, Nicholas found he could see quite a long way by the light of the Milky Way which spread in a wide band across the entire sky.

After they had journeyed for a while, taking a path which wended its way up a precipitous mountain, Nicholas enquired tentatively, 'Are we going far?'

The only response he received was Tai Lo Fu hissing for silence and Ah Kwan murmuring, 'Don't talk. It's dangerous here.'

Not three hundred metres further on Ah Kwan, who was in front, halted abruptly and without any warning. Nicholas, almost colliding with him, was hurriedly pressed down into a crouch by Tai Lo Fu who cocked his sub-machine-gun. The smooth metallic click was ominous and threatening.

Ah Kwan briefly looked over his shoulder, pointed to his ear, then up ahead. Nicholas held his breath. For a moment he could hear nothing but the warm night wind then, no louder than a distant whisper, he heard men talking in low tones.

Ah Kwan and Tai Lo Fu exchanged glances, the latter easing his way by Nicholas. As he passed, he gave him a gentle tap on his shoulder and pursed his lips. For a few seconds, the two men communicated in hurried hand signs then, reaching down, they each scooped up a handful of dirt which they rubbed into their foreheads.

Edging forwards with extreme caution, they placed their feet with infinite care upon the path, watching they did not tread on a twig or loose stone. Nicholas, following their example, quickly smeared a little soil on his brow and took up the rear. He was not sure if they wanted him to accompany them but, he thought, they had not signalled him to stay back.

Ten metres ahead the path curved around a boulder. Above it, the top of a large tree was just visible. The two men reached the boulder and Ah Kwan inched his head over the top. For a moment, he was quite still then, without turning his head, he signed to Tai Lo Fu who moved up to take a look for himself. Nicholas crept to the side of the boulder and peered round it.

Before him was a Japanese patrol. The soldiers were sitting on the ground underneath the tree. Several smoked thin cigarettes, cupped in their fingers to hide the glow of the tobacco. Leaning against the bank were their rifles. An officer, standing by the tree trunk, was studying a map with a hooded torch, talking in subdued tones to a *gunso*. The scene was, Nicholas thought, like a little tableau being put on for his entertainment.

The officer folded the map, switched off his torch and muttered a curt command. The soldiers stubbed out their cigarette butts but did not discard them: instead, they put them in their pockets. At another murmured command from the *gunso*, they picked up their weapons and started off along the path – towards the boulder and Nicholas. He looked sideways to see what Ah Kwan and Tai Lo Fu were doing.

They were nowhere to be seen.

The Japanese were almost up to the boulder and the path was less than a metre from Nicholas's feet.

His heart was beating like a temple drum, so loud he was certain the Japanese would hear it. He wanted to run but he could not, his feet felt rooted to the spot. His brow erupted in sweat which dribbled bits of dirt into his eyes. He wanted to rub it free but could not move his arms. Invisible manacles held him as tight as a strait-jacket.

The first Japanese soldier appeared round the boulder. He was so close that, by the starlight, Nicholas could clearly define his soft-peaked field cap, its leather chin strap and the buckles on his belt. No sooner had he moved on than another appeared. Nicholas closed his eyes. He could not watch the terrifying procession.

The Japanese patrol was gone in less than ninety seconds but, to Nicholas, it seemed like ninety minutes during which time, at any moment, he expected to hear a voice grunt and a rifle butt punch into his chest. When something finally did touch him, he jumped and sucked his breath in so hard it hurt.

It was Ah Kwan, grinning widely in the starlight. Behind him stood Tai Lo Fu. He, too, was grinning.

'You are a good soldier,' Tai Lo Fu whispered. 'You keep your head when it is dangerous. But,' he added, his smile waning, 'next time you must watch what we do.'

Before dawn, they reached a mountain pass and rested for an hour in a dense patch of scrub, in the centre of which had been constructed a small roof of leaves and twigs and a square of tarpaulin.

'Is this your camp?' Nicholas enquired. It did not look much like a base from which to attack the Japanese army.

'No,' Ah Kwan explained, stretching out on the ground. 'This is just a safe place to hide. It's dangerous to walk in the first light of day. If you are seen walking when dawn comes, and the Japanese find you, they think you have walked all night. And that makes them ask questions. So we stop here until the sun is high.'

Nicholas settled himself on the ground and fell asleep to dream of Japanese soldiers who stepped over him, and trod on him, and looked at him, but did not see him because he was invisible.

The sun was well up when they left the hide-out to descend towards the sea and a fishing hamlet in a sandy bay. As they approached it, people working in a few fields by a stream waved. Ah Kwan and Tai Lo Fu returned the greeting. Half a dozen others, working on an upturned sampan on the beach, put down their tools and hurried towards the houses from which a number of other men appeared, several carrying rifles.

Within minutes of their arrival, food was produced by three young women, one of whom wore an olive green cap with a red star embroidered on the front. As they ate, Ah Kwan and Tai Lo Fu reported their encounter with the enemy patrol. The men, all of them looking like peasant farmers and fishermen, paid close attention. Nicholas paid little attention to anything but his food. Until now, he had not realized how hungry he was and he quickly devoured his serving even though he was not in the least fond of the congee rice porridge he was given.

'Who are all these men, Ah Kwan?' Nicholas asked as the meal came to an end.

'All these men,' Ah Kwan said proudly, 'are the East River Column fighters.'

'What are their names?'

'We do not use our names.'

Tai Lo Fu finished speaking and Nicholas became aware that all the men were looking at him now, smiling and talking animatedly amongst themselves.

'What did Tai Lo Fu say to them?' he asked.

'He told them you are a boy, but you are also a brave soldier. Not someone who runs away. Like a chicken.' Ah Kwan flapped his elbows. '*Buk! Buk! Buk!* Lay an egg!'

A few of the men laughed at this, yet they were still serious. They knew – and Nicholas now realized – that had he panicked neither Ah Kwan nor Tai Lo Fu would now be alive: and he would be, at best, a prisoner of war.

Nicholas put down his bowl and spoon and, imitating Ah Kwan, said in Cantonese, '*Buk! Buk! Buk!* I sound like a chicken but I don't run.'

At this all the men roared with mirth and one of them rested his hand on Nicholas's shoulder in a brotherly fashion. When the raucous laughter subsided, he leaned towards Nicholas and said, 'You cannot be told my name, but you know my child. I am Qing-mai's father.'

Nicholas looked at him and replied solemnly, 'I know Qing-mai well. We live together at Sek Wan and she is my good friend.'

'How is she?'

'She is well and happy.'

Everyone fell silent. Qing-mai's father stood up and bowed to Nicholas who, feeling it was the correct thing to do, returned the courtesy to the murmured approval of the whole assembly.

When the meal was over, Nicholas was taken along the shore to a point where a number of trees hung out over the beach. Under their canopy, safe from prying eyes, two of the partisans dug in the sand and pulled out a metal British army ammunition box painted khaki with yellow lettering stencilled upon it. They snapped the catch on the lid and raised it. Inside were a number of cardboard boxes, some packets wrapped in shiny brown greased paper and a manila envelope.

Nicholas took out the envelope and slit it open with his finger. He found a sheet of typed paper. The heading read: *H/E priming and firing instructions (plastic explosive)*.

'Can you do it?' asked Ah Kwan. 'Do you understand it?'

Nicholas did not reply but took the instructions and sat on the sand beside the box. The sunlight filtering through the branches dappled the paper. Gradually, he worked his way through the sheet, identifying first the contents of the ammunition box. These consisted of packets of explosive, detonators, a roll of thin twin-flex wire and several square batteries. This done, he read the instructions on how to prime the explosive with a detonator, wire it up and connect the detonator to the battery. It would have been easier, he thought, if there had been a few diagrams but, in their absence, he believed he had it worked out.

The whole partisan unit, including the young women, gathered under the tree, sitting on the sand in a semicircle. Nicholas stood in front of them, feeling important and wondering if this was what it was like to be a teacher in front of a class.

'This box,' he began, hoping his Cantonese was up to the task, 'contains what the British army calls HE. This means,' he reverted momentarily to English, 'High Explosive.'

Several of the partisans repeated '*aich ee*' parrot-fashion, like children learning their tables and Nicholas, glancing about his audience, realized that some of Tai Lo Fu's soldiers were teenagers, only a few years older than himself.

'This,' Nicholas demonstrated, holding up the contents of the box item by item, 'is HE. This is a . . .' He had no idea what the Cantonese was for 'detonator'. 'This is

62

called in English a detonator. It makes the HE explode. This is detonator-connecting wire and this is a . . .' again, he had to use English '. . . a battery to set the detonator off.'

'In Cantonese, it is called *din chi*,' called out one of the partisans.

Nicholas smiled his thanks and repeated the word. Another partisan said, 'You teach us *aich ee*, we teach you Cantonese.'

Everyone laughed. Nicholas joined in yet, at the same time, he realized this was no laughing matter. Before him in the ammunition box was sufficient explosive to blow them all sky high.

Nicholas unwrapped a block of explosive which had the consistency of putty. He inserted a detonator into it and connected the wires up. Then he explained how, on contact with the battery, the detonator – which he now translated as *pao cheung*, or firecracker – would blow the charge.

When Nicholas's lecture was over, Tai Lo Fu proposed they try it out. Cutting off a small piece of explosive the size of a matchbox from the block, he led the partisans to the far end of the beach where there was a tumble of boulders near the mouth of a stream. Here, he selected a crevice, pressing the explosive into it. This done, he pushed a detonator into it and, connecting the wires, ran them back along the beach for fifty metres. When everything was set and all the partisans had either taken cover behind the trees or lain down flat on the beach, Tai Lo Fu took hold of the battery and connected one wire to the negative terminal. After pausing dramatically for a moment, he touched the other wire against the positive terminal.

There was a sharp report. Splinters of stone sprayed out into the sea. A small cloud of sand rose and fell in the air. The partisans rose to their feet or came out from behind the trees and looked at each other with obvious delight.

When the wire was rolled up and the battery put away, Tai Lo Fu addressed the partisans and Nicholas.

'We thank you for teaching us,' Tai Lo Fu announced. 'You are not only a good soldier like us but also a clever boy. Now we have *aich ee*, we can go to Kowloon and make plenty of trouble for the Japanese.' He paused and turned directly to face Nicholas. 'Now you are one of us. You are an East River Column soldier, a Tai Lo Fu soldier. I ask you to come with us, to see us make trouble for the Japanese.'

'What kind of trouble?' Nicholas replied.

'Big trouble!' Tai Lo Fu explained. 'Now we have *aich ee*, we can strike at a primary target.'

There was a murmur of anticipation in the ranks of the partisans.

'Now,' Tai Lo Fu continued, 'we can hit the Kowloon to Canton railway.'

For a moment, Nicholas wondered if he had heard correctly. Tai Lo Fu was suggesting he might go with the partisans and actually blow up a train.

*

At midday, the men set to cleaning their weapons and studying maps of Hong Kong. A detachment of four men, including Qing-mai's father, left the camp and made off in the direction of the pass. Nicholas watched them go, amazed at the speed with which they ascended the steep slope.

'When do I return to Sek Wan?' Nicholas enquired as the last of the party vanished.

'Later,' Ah Kwan declared. 'It is not safe for you to go now. The Japanese we saw in the night are still in the mountains. Now,' he went on, 'we do not have much to eat here. Will you help us fish?'

Nicholas agreed and Ah Kwan gave him a weighted line wound on to a carved wooden spindle. He suggested Nicholas should fish from the rocks near the stream as shoals of big garoupa gathered around there.

'What do I use for bait?' Nicholas asked.

'Come,' Ah Kwan replied, 'and I will show you.'

He went to within a few metres of the water's edge then, squatting down, frantically dug around a tiny burrow in the damp sand. His hole was just beginning to fill with water when he snatched at the sand and held out a small translucent crab waving its claws indignantly in mid-air, its legs scratching to gain a hold on Ah Kwan's fingers. Taking the line from Nicholas, he pushed the hook through the crab's carapace and let it dangle from his hand.

'This is how you throw the line,' Ah Kwan went on, swinging it round his head, paying a little out at a time. 'Do not be too quick or the crab falls off.'

When he had four metres of line circling his head, Ah Kwan let it go. The line stripped off the spindle and the weight dropped into the sea twenty metres out. He reeled the line in and Nicholas attempted a cast, but he could only reach half as far as Ah Kwan had done.

'No need to worry,' Ah Kwan assured him. 'The fish come close to the rocks. You can catch them easily. But,' he cautioned, 'be careful. Do not swim or fall in the sea. The water is very deep, very fast. If you fall in . . .' he made his hand fly through the air '. . . you will not come back.'

Promising to watch his step and not to swim, Nicholas set off for the rocks. He paused on the way to collect half a dozen crabs which he put in his pocket for safe keeping. He could feel their legs scrabbling against the material. Finding a flat area to stand on, Nicholas baited his hook and cast the line, taking care not to lose his balance. As the weight sank, the current quickly took the line away to his left.

At first, he had grand visions of returning to Sek Wan with a few huge fish dangling from a pole but the garoupa were wily. Several times, Nicholas saw them as huge silver flickers in the deep water but he could not hook one. By mid-afternoon, he had lost the six crabs without so much as hooking a single fish. The sun was high and he was getting both bored and thirsty. When the last crab was snatched from the hook, he decided he had had enough and began to reel the line in.

Just as the hook broke the surface, Nicholas happened to glance out to sea. In the distance, a grey shape moved along the horizon, indistinct in the heat haze. A thin plume of smoke smudged the sky.

A voice shouted from along the beach. Nicholas turned. Ah Kwan was running towards the rocks, his bare feet kicking up sprays of sand.

'Japanese! Run!' he yelled.

Nicholas looked back out to sea. The grey shape was suddenly much larger and had taken on the form of a gunboat. Even though it was still some way offshore, Nicholas could clearly define the superstructure and the naval cannon mounted on the foredeck.

He dropped the fishing line and scrambled down the rocks, barking his shin painfully. The moment he hit the sand, Ah Kwan grabbed his arm and sped with him for the cover of some trees just across a tidal pool at the head of the beach.

Crouched in the shade, Nicholas glanced at the hamlet. Two of the women were sitting at a tub laundering clothes. Nearby, a man chopped kindling whilst, a little way off by the upturned sampan, three others scraped weed and barnacles off its hull. One man was checking fishing nets drying on a wooden frame. Of the rest of the partisan unit there was not a sign.

'Where is Tai Lo Fu?' Nicholas asked.

'In a hole,' Ah Kwan answered enigmatically. 'Like a rabbit.'

A hundred metres offshore, the gunboat slowed. The bow dropped and the hull came side on to the beach. Nicholas, lying next to Ah Kwan on the sandy ground, could see sailors moving on the deck. At the stern hung the Japanese flag, the red sun and its rays stark against a white background.

The men by the sampan put down their tools and waved to the Japanese in a friendly manner. The man at the fishing nets followed their example.

'Why hasn't everyone gone to the hole?' Nicholas whispered.

'If the Japanese see no people,' Ah Kwan replied, 'they will send an armed patrol ashore to look around. If there are a few people, the Japanese do not worry. They think this is just a small village for fishermen. Now, no more talking.'

A dinghy was lowered. Four Japanese sailors rowed to the shore and approached the sampan. They had rifles but kept them slung over their shoulders. For a few minutes, there was a brief conversation during which the Japanese raised their voices and the man with the nets was slapped hard in the face. Recovering from the blow, he ran up to the houses to return with a bag of woven grass. He handed it to one of the Japanese, bowing to him as he did so. The Japanese looked in it and shrugged, then slapped the man once more for good measure before ordering his companions into their dinghy. In a few minutes, they had rowed back to the gunboat. Nicholas and Ah Kwan, still keeping their heads down, could hear the winch raise the dinghy aboard. It was followed by the beat of the marine diesels as the vessel slowly turned out to sea, accelerated and sailed out of sight around the headland beyond the rocks.

'What was in the bag?' Nicholas asked as he rose to his feet.

Ah Kwan answered, 'Dried fish.'

'If you have so little food,' Nicholas reasoned, 'why did the men give them fish? Couldn't they give something else?'

'The Japanese wanted food,' Ah Kwan replied. He burst out laughing and added, 'Tonight, the Japanese sailors will be very sick.' He mimicked vomiting, racking his throat. 'We have put poisonous herbs in them.'

As the sun set behind the mountains and Nicholas made ready for his journey back to Sek Wan, Qing-mai's father and the rest of his detachment returned. Tired and quiet, they went straight to report to Tai Lo Fu who seemed pleased with the account of their patrol. He dismissed them but whereas the others went off to the houses, Qing-mai's father approached Nicholas. He held out a small square of paper which Nicholas noticed was torn from the lining of the explosives box. Upon it were scrawled some characters in pencil.

'Please,' Qing-mai's father said, pressing the paper into Nicholas's hand, 'give this to Qing-mai. Tell her her father thinks of her. Every day.'

As the twilight deepened, Ah Kwan and Nicholas left the hamlet. Tai Lo Fu personally said goodbye to Nicholas and, once again, made a little speech in which he said he hoped Nicholas would join his brave soldiers to fight against the evil enemy.

At the pass, Nicholas paused to look back at the hamlet below. An oil lamp shone in front of the houses. Out to sea, billowing cumulus clouds showed ghostly white in the last of the daylight. It all looked so peaceful and serene, a timeless panorama in which it was hard for Nicholas to believe there was, hidden in the trees and fields, enough explosives to blow up a train. Or more.

Following mountain paths, Ah Kwan made no attempt at caution. Even when the moon rose, bathing the hillside in grey light, he showed no regard for prudence. He whistled or hummed, occasionally chatted about the birds and animals of the mountains, made no effort to muffle his steps and even carried his rifle with a certain nonchalance. Compared to the outward journey, he was being positively reckless. This worried Nicholas.

'Shouldn't we be a little quieter?' he asked at length.

'There are no Japanese here,' Ah Kwan rejoined confidently, interrupting his humming to speak.

They crossed a ridge where the path descended parallel to a rocky gully interspersed with dense bushes.

'What about the patrol we saw last night?' Nicholas warned.

Ah Kwan stepped off the path and down into the gully. Nicholas descended after him. It was three or four metres deep and ten wide. From between the boulders came the musical tinkle of a mountain brook. Ah Kwan pushed some bushes aside. Beneath them, by the light of the moon, Nicholas could make out what appeared at first to be several large bundles; then, like someone looking at a trick puzzle, his eyes came to understand what they were looking at. A hand glowed with a pale sheen in the moonlight.

'Qing-mai's father was busy here,' Ah Kwan said bluntly.

He let the bushes go. They sprang back into place. For a few moments, Nicholas heard a low droning sound. It might, he thought, be one of the Japanese still alive and moaning.

Despite his being the enemy, a pang of pity for the injured man ran through Nicholas. Yet, at the same time, a bolt of fear struck him: the soldier might still be in possession of his rifle and the moonlight was clear enough to shoot by. What was more, the wounded man would be in the shadow and Nicholas was standing above him, a clear target. Yet Ah Kwan seemed quite unconcerned. He had his back to the bushes and was clambering up to the rim of the gully.

The droning subsided. Nicholas followed Ah Kwan but, as he gained the path, his foot dislodged a large stone which rolled down into the bushes. The noise began again, louder.

Something heavy hit his arm just above his wrist and stuck there.

Looking down, Nicholas saw a huge bluebottle sitting on his skin, its polished black thorax shining like leaded metal in the moonlight.

'Flies,' Ah Kwan said. 'There are plenty of flies in the bushes. Laying their eggs on dead Japanese.'

Nicholas swatted it away with his hand, a vision forming in his mind. It was like a short film, the sort he had seen in the cinema before the main picture came on. In it, he watched as the fly left the open eye of a dead Japanese soldier, flew through the air and landed on his own face, moving towards his lips.

A surge of bile rose to Nicholas's throat. He thought he was going to vomit and leaned forward. He retched but nothing came. Only a dribble of saliva hung from his mouth. Ah Kwan put a consoling arm around his shoulders.

'The first time I was very sick,' he said comfortingly as he pulled a water bottle out of his knapsack and handed it to Nicholas. 'You take a drink. Wash out your mouth, but do not swallow.'

When Nicholas felt better, they continued down the path. For the next two hours, until they reached Sek Wan, Nicholas did not speak. He kept thinking of how close those men had passed to him only twenty-four hours ago and how, now, they were all dead and food for maggots.

*

Nicholas arrived back at Sek Wan not long after dawn. He had travelled the last kilometre or so alone, as Ah Kwan had parted from him near the bridge over the creek. He was heading off in the direction of Kowloon, following orders from Tai Lo Fu to look at the railway line.

Entering through the gatehouse, the first thing Nicholas did was find Qing-mai. She was in the main house, helping Venerable Grandmother lay a new fire in the stove.

'I have a message for you,' he said, taking the square of paper out of his pocket. 'It's from your father. I met him.'

Qing-mai took the paper. Her hand shook slightly.

'Thank you, Wing-ming,' she said. 'How is my father?'

'He is very well,' Nicholas reported, 'and he said for me to tell you he thinks of you every day.'

'And I think of him,' she replied with a catch in her voice. She sat at the table and read the letter slowly, savouring every word.

When Tang returned from preparing the sampan for the day's fishing, Nicholas decided to broach the subject of Tai Lo Fu's suggestion that he join the partisans. Tang made no immediate response but, from the moment Nicholas finished speaking, Ah Mee was steadfast.

'You no can go,' she said adamantly. 'Very danger for you. This no play game.'

'No,' replied Nicholas, thinking of the crumpled bodies in the gully and hearing again the hum of the flies busy at their awful labour. 'I know.'

There was an uneasy silence. Nicholas knew what was on Ah Mee's mind. She felt a responsibility for him not only because she had taken care of him in the absence of his parents but also because she loved him.

Tang cleared his throat and said, 'Yes, war no game. But,' he looked at Ah Mee, 'if Tai Lo Fu say he want Wing-ming to fight, then he must go. This war not just English people and Chinese people fighting Japanese people. It is good people fighting bad people. We are good people. It is our job to fight evil.'

He paused and looked from one member of his family to the other. Laan Doh Mao the cat came in the doorway, miaowed and jumped on to Venerable Grandmother's lap, snuggling down as the old woman's gnarled fingers stroked between the purring animal's shoulders.

'Not all Japanese are bad,' Tang continued. 'Some are good people. In Sai Kung, there is a Japanese soldier who is very kind. He does not hit people, does not take fish without paying. But others are bad. And we must fight them. Chinese boy fight, so why not English boy?' His gaze fixed on Nicholas. 'If you go with Tai Lo Fu, much danger for you. But if you want go, you go.' He paused then added, 'My father and mother think you their Number One Grandson. Ah Mee like your mother. You all same my Number One Son. We love you, Nicholas Wing-ming, and we afraid for you. But we not stop you. You no small boy now. You half-man.'

Nicholas left the room. Laan Doh Mao followed in his footsteps. By the temple door, Dai Kam the dog lay on his side, snoozing in the warm sun. The cat glanced lazily around then set off towards the gatehouse to lie upon the roof, dozing and waiting for an unwary bird to land on the ridge.

An itch started in between Nicholas's shoulder-blades. It was if someone was watching him. He turned. From the dark interior of the temple, the white porcelain face of Tin Hau gazed placidly out from beneath her head-dress of red silk.

Stepping over the raised sill, Nicholas entered the temple. The oil lamp guttered by the pillar. Six joss-sticks, one for each member of the family including Nicholas, curled their smoke into the soot-blackened rafters. Venerable Grandmother made sure they were lit every morning. On a dish in front of the goddess was a dried fish by way of an offering.

Nicholas stared at the idol. She stared back. Her eyes were emotionless but a faint smile played on her lips. She seemed to offer some blessing in return for the fish which, although he had not placed it there, was the result of his daily work.

'What do you think, Tin Hau?' Nicholas asked, despite himself. 'You think I should go?'

The joss-stick smoke rose and the flame flickered. Then, to Nicholas's utter astonishment, someone said, 'Yes.'

Nicholas started.

'That's silly,' he said to himself. 'Tin Hau can't talk. She's a wooden statue.'

The voice repeated itself. It did not speak in an ordinary voice but lingered on the ending to the word, turning the *s* into a sort of elongated *th*.

Yeth-th-th-th.

Nicholas was determined to discover the source of the voice. As he stepped to one side of the altar and peered round the back of the idol, he half expected to find Qing-mai behind the statue playing a trick on him. Behind the altar, there was a small space between it and the rear wall in which Venerable Grandmother kept bundles of joss-sticks, a few wooden tablets carved with the names of her ancestors and a pot of red paint to spruce up the temple pillars.

The only light to reach the space came from a tiny grilled window high up in the wall, through which the joss-stick smoke drifted into the sky. Even that light was softly green from the fronds of bamboo which grew close to the buildings.

Nicholas could see nothing. Certainly, no one was hiding there. Yet, just as he turned away, the voice spoke again, loudly, more insistently.

'*Yeth-th-th-th*,' it declared, then repeated itself for emphasis. '*Yeth-th-th-th*.'

It was easier to pinpoint the direction of the sound now so Nicholas took hold of the altar lamp and, cautiously, entered the space. Lying on the smooth flagstones was a snake over a metre long. Its body was curled, but its head was raised up, its neck spread out into a hood. The reptile's underside was pale cream with two faint black bands a few centimetres below the throat. Nicholas knew what it was: he had seen them in the garden at Peony Villa. It was a cobra and highly venomous.

Very slowly, Nicholas began to back off. The snake sensed the motion and hissed again, swaying its head slightly backwards and forwards. Nicholas froze.

If the snake struck, Nicholas knew he was done for. The thought raced through his mind: if quinine, which had been so common before the war, was so difficult to buy now then snake-bite serum would be impossible to obtain. Besides, if you were bitten, you had to have the serum injected within thirty minutes.

While Nicholas stood as still as a statue, the snake made no further sound and, after a short while, it deflated the hood on its neck. Satisfied Nicholas posed no threat, the reptile slithered round and disappeared into a hole in the wall which served as a drain.

Nicholas's knees felt weak and his hands shook as he left the temple. Tang, coming out of the house on the way to his sampan, saw him and came over.

'You very white,' he observed. 'You got fever?'

'I've just seen a cobra,' Nicholas said, his voice a little tremulous.

'In temple?' Tang asked.

Nicholas nodded.

'Snake live in temple. Long time. When I was young man, snake there.'

'A cobra can't live that long,' Nicholas retorted.

'Can do,' Tang said. 'Cobra can live thirty year. Bring good luck for my family.'

'I don't see,' Nicholas replied, 'how it can bring good luck.'

'I tell you. This snake live here. We no touch him. He know we no touch him. Dai Kam no go near him, Laan Doh Mao no go near him. He safe here. But this not his house so he must pay us to live here.'

'How can a snake pay you?' Nicholas interjected.

Tang laughed and said, 'Wing-ming, you no understand. You got Chinese name, live with Chinese people, speak Cantonese but you still English in you heart. That good. You must stay English for when the war end. This why I talk English to you all time. Now,' he continued, 'I tell you. Chinese idea sometimes seem crazy to English people. We say snake lucky, and you say that crazy Chinese talk. But Chinese talk not crazy. You think, this snake live here. He pay rent. How? We no touch him, he eat rat and mouse. If he eat rat and mouse, then rat and mouse no eat our rice, no eat our flour, no bite us, no make us sick. So . . .'

'Snake lucky,' Nicholas cut in.

'Snake very lucky,' Tang answered. 'Now I go catch fish.'

Nicholas watched from the terrace as Tang launched the sampan and set off towards the promontory. For the first time, he realized there was substance to Chinese sayings and proverbs. The beliefs must make sense. It was just that the truth behind them was somehow disguised by folklore.

He ran through a few superstitions in his mind. Bats were lucky: they would be good because they ate mosquitoes which could give malaria. It was very unlucky to have a pet cat stolen: that could mean the mice could breed. It was always wise to have a clump of bamboo growing near a house: this would not only provide building materials and poles to carry things on but it would also provide a home for snakes – like the cobra.

If, Nicholas reasoned, there was a sound piece of common sense behind such superstitious beliefs, was there also an argument for accepting omens? Had the snake been a sign? After all, it had said *yeth-th-th-th* long before it saw him. When he was in front of the altar, he was no threat to the reptile. So why had it hissed?

In his room, Nicholas knelt down and pulled his photograph out from its crevice behind the *kang*; ever since the day when the Japanese had come, he had kept it hidden just in case. He wiped the glass, sat down on the doorstep and held it in both hands. The sun played upon the silver frame.

Nicholas gazed hard at the picture. He knew the people in the photograph were his parents but he could not actually picture them in his mind. He had long since forgotten what they really looked like and, try as he might, he could not recall the sound of their voices. The only firm memory he had of them was the photograph he was holding in his hands. This saddened but did not upset him. He had come to terms with their absence and did not miss them. Not exactly. Not any longer.

Yet, as they looked up at him from the photograph, and he looked down on them, he felt the strong tug of love. Wherever they were – and, deep inside himself, he refused to believe they were dead – he knew they were thinking of him, perhaps at that very moment.

'What do you think, Dad?' he asked, out loud.

It was the first time he had ever spoken to the photograph. Feeling a little self-conscious, he looked around to be sure none of the others was in sight. Nothing moved on the terrace, not even Dai Kam. The figures in the silver frame were just as immobile, frozen in time and the chemicals of the photograph.

Yet, as he gazed at the picture, Nicholas heard one sound in his head.

It was *yeth-th-th-th*.

*

Not long after sun-up Nicholas waited, his varnished cane hat in his hands, as Tai Lo Fu and ten other men, including Ah Kwan, arrived at the end of the bridge. None of them looked the least like a fighter: they were more like peasant farmers, fishermen and coolies. One of them even carried a rice flail whilst another had a wooden rake balanced over his shoulder. A third had a basket of woven straw, its top sewn closed with cord. Not one appeared to be armed.

'So you ready to fight?' Tai Lo Fu asked, speaking to Nicholas in English for the first time.

'Yes,' Nicholas said, his voice determined.

'Good! Now you can fight for your father.'

They left the bridge together but, halfway to Sai Kung, they halted and, at Tai Lo Fu's order, split into five separate groups.

'This is for safety,' Ah Kwan explained. 'The Japanese have made a law that no more than three people can walk at one time together. If you see any Tai Lo Fu soldiers today you do not greet them, do not talk to them. You do not know them. You understand?' He looked at Nicholas's hat and added, 'Wear your hat now.'

'I understand,' Nicholas said and, putting on his hat, he joined Tai Lo Fu and Ah Kwan who set off first. They did not walk quickly or even purposefully, but ambled along as if they were out for a stroll. Once, they even stopped to admire the view.

'*Ho leng!*' Tai Lo Fu exclaimed. 'Very beautiful. This why we fight. To keep China looking beautiful.'

At mid-morning, they reached Sai Kung. The fishing village was sleepy in the hot sun. The market was not due to open until the afternoon because the Japanese had done away with the traditional early morning gathering when they had forbidden night fishing.

Tai Lo Fu went towards the tea-shop where Nicholas and Ah Mee had rested on their flight to buy quinine but Ah Kwan guided Nicholas to the shadow of a nearby house.

'We don't drink tea,' he explained. 'Not yet. Wait a few minutes. Tai Lo Fu will talk first.'

The partisan leader sat down at one of the tables standing under a tree and stretched his legs out in front of him. The proprietor with the twisted ear came out but he did not leer or demand that Tai Lo Fu order a bowl of tea. Instead, he gave a short bow and spoke to him in a muted voice. This conversation over, Tai Lo Fu beckoned Ah Kwan and Nicholas to join him.

'No Japanese have been here today,' Tai Lo Fu said in a low voice, 'but they've caught a Wang Ching-wei man.'

'What's a Wang Ching-wei?' Nicholas asked.

'Wang Ching-wei is a bad Chinese man,' Ah Kwan explained. 'He is a friend to the Japanese. His men tell the Japanese what good Chinese people do. They would tell the Japanese that Tai Lo Fu is in Sai Kung today. Then the Japanese would come and kill him.'

The tea-house owner served three bowls of tea, for which he demanded no payment, and handed Tai Lo Fu a two-page propaganda newspaper printed in Chinese but with a Japanese flag above the headline. No one spoke. Ah Kwan leaned back in his chair. Tai Lo Fu read the newspaper, snorting every now and then, muttering, '*Laap saap!*' – which meant 'rubbish' – every time he read a blatant Japanese lie. Two of the partisans approached along the village street, one of them the man with the rake. Nicholas ignored them.

When he had finished his tea, Tai Lo Fu folded the newspaper and called to the tea-house owner. The man closed his business and led them through the village, across some paddyfields and over a stream to a farmhouse surrounded on three sides by trees. Looking around to ensure they were not being observed, the tea-house owner knocked twice on the door. It was immediately opened.

Stepping inside with the men, Nicholas found himself in a large room. Against the walls were piled bamboo canes, farming implements and the remains of a cart. The air smelled cool and fusty. From a doorway at the rear came a grunting sound. It reminded Nicholas of the pigs at Sek Wan.

Following Tai Lo Fu through the door, he discovered this sound came not from a pig but a man. Wearing only a pair of shorts, he had been tied to an old cart wheel with his arms and legs outspread. His body was covered in bruises and cuts, and his face was badly swollen. His chest was slick and shiny with sweat and blood. In front of him stood two other men stripped to the waist. One held a stout bamboo pole.

'This is the Wang Ching-wei man,' Ah Kwan said. 'He is a traitor.'

Tai Lo Fu moved in front of the prisoner and, putting his head close to the swollen face, asked a question in Cantonese, in a soft, wheedling voice. He sounded almost like a child trying to coax one more sweet out of a parent who thought it had had enough.

The prisoner muttered something. Tai Lo Fu leaned forward. The prisoner repeated what he said. Tai Lo Fu smiled ironically then stepped back.

'You understand English?' Tai Lo Fu enquired.

The prisoner attempted to speak but he could only mumble.

'I tell you something, Wang Ching-wei man,' Tai Lo Fu declared, speaking now in English. 'Japanese no can win war. We win. Communist fighter win. Chinese people win.' He leaned towards the prisoner. 'You want know why I talk English. I tell you. You see this boy?' Tai Lo Fu turned, taking Nicholas by the hand, drawing him nearer the prisoner and removing his hat. 'You tell him you name,' he ordered.

'My name is Wing-ming,' Nicholas announced in Cantonese.

'No,' Tai Lo Fu said. 'You tell you real name. Speak in English.'

'My name is Nicholas,' Nicholas admitted, not wanting to look at the prisoner yet staring at him with a fascination he could not control.

'This,' Tai Lo Fu went on grandly, 'is English boy. Live Hong Kong all time you Japanese friend here. He fighter for me, bring my men good luck.' His voice changed. 'I know what you say. You say, if Tai Lo Fu got English boy, how many English men he got? I tell you. I got plenty men. In China. Chinese men, English men, American men. We got gun, we got airplane, we got bomb. One day, no long time, Wang Ching-wei no more. Japanese soldier no more.'

He let go of Nicholas's hand and raised his arm. Nicholas thought he was going to strike the prisoner. The prisoner also thought so and flinched in anticipation of the blow. Tai Lo Fu lowered his arm and laughed humourlessly before turning away to speak briefly in Cantonese to the two guards.

They left the building then and returned across the paddyfield. For some way, Nicholas was silent, shocked at what he had seen. He knew what was going to happen. Tai Lo Fu had spoken in English because the traitor would not live to report Nicholas's presence.

As the sun went down, they reached the outskirts of Kowloon. They approached it not from the direction by which Nicholas and Ah Mee had come, down the road in the lorry, but over a pass in the Nine Dragon

Mountains which ran east to west along the northern edge of the town.

The climb up to the pass had been hard going but the descent was worse. Tai Lo Fu and Ah Kwan had not kept to paths but, in places, simply made their way downhill in a straight line. Nicholas's legs had ached as he fought against the slope, stopping himself from slipping or being forced into a downhill run he would not be able to check.

They made their way into a ravine filled with bushes in the scrub-covered foothills below the mountains.

'This is where we wait,' Ah Kwan told Nicholas. 'The other men will come soon. You rest now.'

Nicholas leaned back on a smooth rock. He shut his eyes yet did not doze off for his mind remained alert with the anticipation of the mission which lay ahead of them.

Within an hour, the rest of Tai Lo Fu's men arrived. The one carrying the woven basket opened it to produce some bottles of water, buns of steamed bread and thin strips of stringy dried meat which were handed round. Nicholas found the meat tough but, if chewed for some minutes until it softened, delicious.

'What meat is this?' he asked Ah Kwan who was chewing a length of it with obvious relish.

'*Mah lo*,' Ah Kwan informed him.

'*Mah lo?*' Nicholas repeated. The words rang a bell but he could not remember the meaning.

'Monkey,' Ah Kwan said. 'It will make you strong.' He flexed his biceps muscle to prove the point.

'Maybe make you like a monkey,' Nicholas replied and, twisting his arm around, he scratched under his armpit in a simian fashion. The men chuckled quietly at this antic.

'You are a funny boy!' Tai Lo Fu remarked. 'It is good you make us laugh. Soon, we shall not be laughing but fighting.'

Once they had eaten and drunk the water, which was tepid from being in the basket all day, Tai Lo Fu brought out an oblong of paper upon which had been drawn a rough map of Kowloon. In the centre of the map was a circle in red ink and, in the centre of the circle, a railway bridge.

So, Nicholas thought, it was not a train they were to sabotage but the whole railway line.

Looking over Ah Kwan's shoulder, Nicholas briefly studied the map. He knew the bridge. It crossed over Waterloo Road not far from King George V School at which he had spent just one term before the Japanese invasion. He had passed under the bridge every day on his way to school, riding in a Number 7 bus, alighting at the stop beyond it.

Until now, Nicholas had scarcely given school a thought. Certainly, he had not missed it. It was not that he disliked his lessons nor that he had no friends. He enjoyed mathematics and geography and had had many friends, although most of them had left Hong Kong for Australia just before the Japanese invaded. Once the enemy had landed and the school closed, he had been out of touch with the world of education. The war had been, in some respects, like the holidays: once they began, memory of school quickly faded. And, he realized, sitting in the ravine surrounded by partisan fighters preparing to sabotage the bridge, he had learnt a lot more about life at Sek Wan than he ever would have in a classroom.

Tai Lo Fu's plan of attack was simple. They would split into two groups. One would deal with the pair of sentries who sometimes guarded the bridge. This group would then provide cover for the smaller explosives party who would get in under the superstructure of the bridge and plant the charge. With this done, they would retreat to a building near by, across Foch Avenue, which ran parallel to the railway line at the foot of the embankment. From there, they would blow the bridge.

82

It all looked so easy but Nicholas was puzzled by one thing. He mentioned it when Tai Lo Fu had finished outlining his plan.

'How can you fight,' Nicholas enquired, 'and blow up a railway bridge if you don't have guns and high explosive?'

Tai Lo Fu grinned and, asking Nicholas to lean forward, moved the rock against which he had been lying. In a hollow behind it were four rifles, six revolvers, an ammunition box and two packets tied up with twine.

'We have them,' he said with a twinkle in his eye then, lifting one of the two packages, he handed it to Nicholas. 'You take this one.'

As the twilight deepened, they moved out of the ravine and headed towards a suburb with wide residential streets where, before the war, rich people had lived. Nicholas was familiar with the area; his parents had had friends who lived there in a house with a swimming pool and a croquet lawn.

Now, he was shocked by the state of general decrepitude. Broken windows were patched up with cardboard or paper, gardens were a riot of weeds or unkempt bushes, lawns had been dug up for paltry-looking vegetable patches, walls were missing chunks of plaster and the streets were pot-holed. In the grounds of one particularly fine house, the tennis court had been turned into a chicken run. A few scrawny hens scratched at the earth in the last of the daylight before joining the rest of their flock in a makeshift hen-house constructed out of a Morris van with flat tyres and a smashed windscreen.

In darkness, the partisans slipped across the road down which Nicholas had fled that fateful Christmas Day. Not far to their right ran the railway line but they did not approach it. According to Ah Kwan, who had reconnoitred all six railway bridges in Kowloon, the first two nearest the mountains were too heavily guarded to make an attack feasible. The third provided no footholds to the steel girders. The fourth, however, was only lightly patrolled: presumably, Nicholas guessed, the Japanese thought this was less likely to be a target because it was farther from the safety of the foothills. Furthermore, there were steps up the railway embankment which might allow access to the underside of the bridge.

The street lights were not working which gave the partisan band added cover. In less than fifteen minutes, they were crouched by a building at the end of Foch Avenue, studying the bridge.

It seemed, to Nicholas, impregnable, consisting of a steel deck with riveted iron sides at least a metre high. The supporting box girders, set into granite abutments at each end, were massive and obviously designed for extra strength.

For some minutes, the partisans kept still. Everyone, including Nicholas, surveyed the bridge for any sign of a sentry. There was none.

'You wait,' Ah Kwan hissed.

He and another man slipped away at a crouch, crossing the road so silently they might have been running on air. In seconds, they were at the foot of the embankment where they paused then mounted the steps by the bridge. A moment later came a tiny, reedy, barely audible whistle.

'Open your package,' Tai Lo Fu whispered.

Nicholas unwrapped his packet. It contained two detonators and a roll of wire.

One of the men took the end of the wire, running across the avenue and up the steps as Nicholas paid it out from the spool which spun in his hands. Meanwhile, Tai Lo Fu unwrapped the explosive and battery from the other packet.

Leaving Nicholas behind to mind the battery and the end of the wire, the remaining men all headed for the bridge. They were not gone long when Ah Kwan returned.

'We have a problem,' he murmured tersely. 'You come.'

Nicholas ran with Ah Kwan to the embankment then up the steps. The problem was soon evident. The explosive had to be fitted to the interior of one of the box girders to maximise the effect of the blast but the inspection hole through which it was to be inserted was not much greater in diameter than a cricket ball. None of the partisans could get his hand through.

'You can do it,' Tai Lo Fu said quietly. 'You have small hands.'

'Take your shoes off,' Ah Kwan whispered. 'Get a better foothold.'

Making no reply, Nicholas removed his shoes and took a lump of the explosive from Tai Lo Fu. It was cold and soft, reminding him of modelling clay. Thrusting it into his pocket, he started to edge his way out along the lip of the girder, using crossbars supporting the track bed above as handholds.

The inspection hole was about two metres out from the granite abutment. Not daring to look down, Nicholas reached it and, with difficulty, extracted the sticky explosive from his pocket. He managed to get it into the hole with one hand whilst holding on with the other.

'Long way in,' hissed a voice in the darkness.

Pressing with his fingers, Nicholas succeeded in getting the explosive to adhere to the top of the girder, using a bolt or rivet as an anchoring point. This done, he returned to Tai Lo Fu and was given yet more explosive and a detonator to which the wires had been connected.

Once more, Nicholas edged out along the girder, feeling with his toes. The metal was cool and reassuringly firm under the skin of his soles. He got to the hole, pressing the rest of the explosive around the first deposit, and was just about to insert the detonator when he heard another faint whistle. At the same moment, above his head, he discerned two sets of footsteps start out across the bridge from the far end. The sound echoed slightly in the hollow girder. He stopped work and kept perfectly still.

The footsteps came nearer. Low voices were interspersed with short, mirthless laughter. The steps halted above him. One voice spoke, briefly followed by a scratching sound like that of a match being struck. Immediately after that came two heavy thumps on the iron plating of the bridge. Something large and dense dropped past Nicholas to thud on the roadway below.

'All safe now.' It was Ah Kwan's voice. 'You ready?'

Nicholas inserted the detonator well into the explosive, threaded the wire around a crossbar to secure it then made his way back to the embankment, taking care not to tangle himself in the wire.

The charge laid, all the partisans retreated to the corner of the building. As he ran, doubled up, across Foch Avenue, Nicholas glanced under the bridge. In the roadway, he could just make out the body of the Japanese sentry thrown off the bridge.

'You have done well.' Tai Lo Fu praised Nicholas in a muted voice and he handed him the battery. 'You light the *pao cheung*.'

For a moment, Nicholas stared from the battery to Tai Lo Fu's face.

'Do it! Quickly!'

His hands trembling with excitement, Nicholas connected the negative wire to the battery. The men crouched down behind the corner of the building.

'Ready?' Nicholas whispered.

Tai Lo Fu gave a thumbs up.

Nicholas touched the remaining wire against the positive terminal. A tiny spark jumped as the connection was made.

For perhaps half a second, nothing happened. The thought flashed through Nicholas's mind that he must have done something wrong.

There was a large roar. The night filled with a sound so deep, so tremendous, so powerful it made the ground shake as if in an earthquake. Bits of plaster showered down on them. Windows shattered. The trees lining the avenue thrashed as if in a typhoon. A vast billow of dust obscured the embankment. Then all was silent save for the last tinkling of falling glass.

Nicholas was numbed by the blast and the enormity of what he had just done.

There was a creaking sound, like a squeaky door being opened slowly. Nicholas stood up. Tai Lo Fu and his men were already gathered in the middle of Waterloo Road. Nicholas followed.

The bridge had not collapsed but the girder had torn free from the granite wall and buckled, causing the track bed to warp badly.

'No trains to Canton tomorrow,' Ah Kwan remarked laconically.

The sound of vehicles suddenly came to them from far off down the road on the other side of the bridge.

The party split up. Several men ran down Foch Avenue. Others disappeared up a hill beyond the bridge. Two raced up the embankment and vanished over the railway line, making for streets across the tracks. Nicholas, Tai Lo Fu and Ah Kwan headed at a sprint down Waterloo Road and into a side road just a few metres from the bus stop Nicholas knew so well. As they turned, he thought how, when the war was over, he would get off the Number 7 bus here on his way to school, look down the road at the bridge and remember this night.

By the time the Japanese arrived, they were all well on their way back to the safety of the foothills.

Part Four
Summer 1944

After the attack on the railway bridge, the Japanese stepped up security. Street patrols were doubled and road blocks were erected at key junctions. The number of platoons operating in the countryside was increased and, several times in the summer and autumn of 1943, Japanese soldiers appeared at Sek Wan. They ransacked the houses as a matter of course even though they did not expect to find any trace of the guerrillas. Sek Wan was too small a settlement to hide a band of brigands and comparatively too accessible, being within easy reach of Sai Kung by sampan or on foot.

Reprisals were taken in Kowloon by the Kempetai, the Japanese military police. They arrested people at random, publicly executing them by way of example or shipping them off to Japan to work as slave labour in coal mines.

Tai Lo Fu, Ah Kwan and the rest of the East River Column left Hong Kong and went into hiding in China. From time to time, Nicholas heard of their exploits through Tang who picked up rumours in Sai Kung when he went to sell his fish. The rumours were often wild and always unsubstantiated. It was said they had severed the railway to Canton further to the north, and Nicholas believed that story. The rumour that they had captured a Japanese warship and were using it to raid passing Japanese cargo ships, however, seemed too far-fetched to be possible.

For Nicholas, his existence returned to the usual round of village life and he virtually forgot his former life before the war. For some peculiar reason, he remembered owning a steam engine that actually worked off steam. Other details were hazy and he could not recall quite how he had spent his days before they were filled with chores.

He fed the pigs and cleaned out the sties, chopped firewood, gutted and dried fish and took his turn at scaring birds off the vegetables: yet he also picked up new skills. When the sow produced a litter of piglets, he helped butcher them, pouring boiling water over their carcasses to make it easier to remove the hair. Venerable Grandmother instructed him how to pickle cabbage and preserve plums, first by soaking them in sea-water until they were puckered up like prunes then drying them in the sun. Venerable Grandfather gave him tuition in the advanced use of the abacus. However, the most intricate and difficult of his new abilities was taught him by Tang.

One evening, Tang returned late from fishing. Ah Mee, fearing another bout of malaria, waited anxiously for him on the shingle. Nicholas was with her. It was almost dark when the sampan finally hove into view and headed for the beach.

Once she saw he was not sick, Ah Mee grew slightly peeved and reproached her husband.

'Why you long time? Wing-ming and me very worried.'

Tang stepped out of the sampan, his trousers rolled up above his knees. Even in the half-light, they could see his legs were drenched in blood.

'*Ay-ah!*' Ah Mee exclaimed, instantly regretting her chiding.

'Are you all right?' Nicholas asked, somewhat puzzled for Tang seemed uninjured.

'Blood not my blood,' Tang replied and he pointed into the well of the sampan.

Nicholas stepped into the waves and peered into the vessel. Lying on the boards was a large shark, its fin sticking up stiffly into the air like a rigid sail. He leaned over and touched the fish. Its flesh was as hard as seasoned wood.

'We got good luck today,' Tang remarked, bending down to wash the blood off. 'Fin make good soup for us. Meat fetch good money in Sai Kung. But also, we got bad luck.'

He leaned over the side of the sampan and pulled out his fishing net. The shark had bitten large holes in it.

That night, after the shark had been butchered and lightly salted to prevent it going bad, Tang called Nicholas over to him.

'I teach you something,' he said. 'My father show me long time before. He learn from his father. Now I – you Chinese father – teach you.'

Taking up a large ball of tarred cord, he spent the next hour showing Nicholas how to weave and knot a fishing net. It was difficult for they had to work by the light of the oil lamp yet, by ten o'clock, Nicholas had more or less mastered the intricate crossings-over and tuckings-under, and he understood the difference between a tensioning and a sliding knot.

Once Nicholas had acquired the knack, he and Tang talked as they laboured. The others had retired to their *kangs*.

'How long do you think the war will go on?' Nicholas asked after some minutes of silence.

Tang paused and thought before replying. 'Not finish yet. But I think not too long. Maybe one year.'

'Why do you think that?'

'I think because Japanese soldier getting . . .' Tang paused again to gather his reasons. 'I tell you, Wing-ming,' he went on, 'life no so good for Japanese. Soldier get tired. He no like live Hong Kong long time. No can go back his family in Japan. And in Hong Kong, life bad for everybody now.'

He completed a square in the net, his fingers snapping the cord tight. Nicholas sensed a touch of anger or frustration in his action.

'Chinese people say,' Tang continued, starting on a new square '"No money, no talk." This mean if you no got money you no can do anything. People in Hong Kong no got food, no got job, no got money. In Hong Kong, many people die because no food.'

'But we have food,' Nicholas said, 'and you catch fish and sell it. Surely the people who buy your fish . . .'

'Not so many people. Two year before, I sell fish easy. People got money, got gold. Now, people no got money, no got gold. He try to sell other things to buy fish.'

Tang stood and trimmed the wick in the oil lamp, turning it up. The flame had been flickering down and getting smoky. When he sat down again, his face was grim.

'I tell you something,' he said, 'I no tell Ah Mee. Not even my father. I tell you, but you no tell?'

'I won't,' Nicholas promised.

'Last week, when I go to Sai Kung, man come to me. He say, "I no got money. If you give me fish, I give you my jacket." I say no want jacket. I got jacket. This man say, "I give you shoes." I look at his shoes. They are very dirty, very old. Got holes. I say no. Man say, "I give you my wife."'

'What did he mean?' Nicholas asked.

'He mean, if I give him fish to eat, he give me his wife,' Tang answered bluntly. 'He life so bad, he give away his wife be servant f̶ ̶ ̶me so he can eat.'

'What did you

'I give him fish. ̶e say thank you but he look down. Very ashamed. I say, "If you hungry, never mind. No give you family away." He say to me, "I sell my daughter already." Then he cry.'

Nicholas looked at Tang's face. His lips were pursed in a thin line.

'I tell you this because you no more small boy,' Tang said. 'You young man now, must know these things. We very lucky here. Got our field, got our pig, can catch fish. But you no tell Ah Mee, Qing-mai, my parents. I no want them worry, no want them know how bad life in Hong Kong.'

'I'll keep my promise,' Nicholas assured him.

Tang's face lightened a little and he continued, 'I hear one story. Man tell me plenty American airplane in China. Make ready fight Japanese.'

It was past midnight when they finally completed repairing the net. Nicholas helped Tang carry it down to the sampan. There was no moon but the sky was cloudless and the whole of the heavens was a vast panoply of stars. The tide was coming in. The sampan bobbed slightly with its keel still on the shingle, little waves lapping at the polished hull.

When they had the net safely stowed in the bow, Tang said, 'You watch. I show you something.'

He picked up a pebble from the beach and tossed it into the sea. Where it splashed there was a small, momentary explosion of ghostly green light on the surface of the water.

'How did you do that!' Nicholas exclaimed.

Tang threw a larger pebble. The sea erupted with green light once more, the ripples fanning out from the splash, carrying blotches of green light with them which gradually faded.

'Is no trick. You can do,' Tang said.

Nicholas picked up a stone the size of a hen's egg and bowled it underarm over the sea. It curved through the air and struck the water. The green light phosphoresced in the darkness.

'Every year, when the sea warm,' Tang said, 'you can do this. Green light make by very small animal. So small you no can see him.'

Long after Tang had returned to the house, Nicholas remained on the beach, skimming flat stones over the sea, watching the green light magically shine and thinking about the man who wanted to exchange his wife for a few dried fish.

*

One morning in August, Nicholas was working in the fields, hoeing weeds from between the rows of cabbages and diverting water from the stream to irrigate the plants, when Tang appeared at the edge of the trees.

'Wing-ming,' he said, his voice tense and curt. 'You come!'

Nicholas apprehensively followed Tang down the path through the trees. Something was wrong. He could sense it but he was afraid to ask what it was.

A table had been set up under the shade of the lychee tree. Seated at it were two visitors, one with a leather satchel at his feet. Before them were bowls of tea and a dish of Nicholas's preserved salted plums.

As Nicholas approached along the terrace, one of the men left the table and came quickly towards him. It was Ah Kwan.

'*Nei ho ma*, Wing-ming?' he greeted Nicholas, holding out his hand and making a little bow. 'How are you? Long time no see you,' he added in English.

Nicholas shook his hand and returned the bow, saying, 'I am well.'

'I been live in China,' Ah Kwan said, still in English. 'Place called Waichow.'

'How is Tai Lo Fu?'

'Tai Lo Fu good. No live China now. Live Hainan Island.'

'Did you and Tai Lo Fu capture a Japanese warship?' Nicholas wanted to know.

Ah Kwan laughed and said, 'This funny story people say because Tai Lo Fu big-time leader.' He beckoned to Nicholas. 'I want you meet my friend.'

The second visitor stood up and turned around, saying in perfect English, 'So you're the famous Nicholas Holford. I've heard a lot about you and I'm delighted to meet you.'

Nicholas, who had half bowed to the man on the assumption he was Chinese, gaped at him. He was of average height, dressed in a loose Chinese jacket and nondescript trousers. His hair was black, his eyes were dark and his skin was tanned. He might have been a local peasant – but he was English.

'This Major Fox,' Ah Kwan introduced him. 'He English officer, live Waichow.'

'I'm sure you're somewhat taken aback,' Major Fox said.

'I've not met an English person for a long time,' Nicholas replied.

In his mind, he tried to work out how long it had been, but he could neither work out the length of time he had lived in Sek Wan nor who the last English person he had spoken to might have been. He was not even sure if it was one of his parents.

'Indeed not,' Major Fox answered. 'And I'm sure you did not expect the next one to be dressed up like a rickshaw driver.'

'I'm not . . .' Nicholas began, then he stopped.

He was suddenly unsure of himself. He had escaped through occupied Hong Kong, gone on the mission to fetch quinine and been within a hair's breadth of being captured by a Japanese patrol. He had learnt how to set a charge, blow up a bridge and mend a net and yet, before this officer, one of his own kind – his own people – he felt inexplicably ill at ease.

'Don't worry,' Major Fox said, smiling. 'I must be quite a shock. Please, come and sit down.'

Nicholas sat at the table next to Ah Kwan. He felt safer, more at ease, with the partisan than the Englishman.

'Let me tell you a little about myself,' Major Fox suggested. 'You will, of course, keep what I say secret. I know from Kwan here you are not a blabber-mouth.' He sipped his tea, put the bowl down and went on, 'I am a British army major posted to Waichow with an organization called the British Army Aid Group. BAAG for short.'

Nicholas half smiled. Major Fox pronounced the acronym like 'bag' but with a sheep-like bleat in the centre.

'We have two main roles,' the major continued. 'The first is to gather information from partisan fighters like Kwan and Tai Lo Fu and send this back to our HQ in Chungking. We supply them with arms, ammunitions and explosives in return. The plastic explosive for which you translated the notes came from me.'

'They didn't understand what to do with it,' Nicholas remarked.

Major Fox grinned a little sheepishly and said, 'Yes. That was rather stupid of me. All deliveries since then have had instructions in Chinese.' He sipped his tea before going on. 'Our second role is to be in touch with and support prisoners of war. As I'm sure you know from your visit to Kowloon to buy medicine, the situation there is far from jolly. People are near starving. In the prison camps, it is far, far worse. The Japanese withhold medical supplies, issue only the most basic and poorest quality of foodstuffs, give out no clothing or bedding. What is worse, the men are forced to work long hours, regardless of the weather, labouring to build the airport.'

'You remember?' Ah Kwan cut in. 'You see me when you go Kowloon with Ah Mee. I no coolie. I pretend I coolie. Can talk to prisoner, take him something.'

In his mind, Nicholas recalled the hand clamped on his shoulder, the Japanese shadows on the ground, Ah Mee fainting and Ah Kwan, caked with sweat and dust.

'Kwan has not only been fighting with Tai Lo Fu,' Major Fox explained. 'He has also been what we call "playing music on the bamboo radio".'

'What does that mean?' Nicholas asked. He had never heard of a radio made out of bamboo.

'It's code,' the major said, 'a sort of slang for secret messages. The information and news Kwan smuggles to the prisoners in the camps is like music to their ears. It boosts their morale, lets them know they are not forgotten. Sometimes news can be a better tonic than medicine. Medicine just cures your ills but news can give you hope. The network in which Kwan operates we jokingly call the bamboo radio.'

'I've not had any news for a long time,' Nicholas said.

'Then let me give you some,' Major Fox replied. 'In Europe, the Nazis are being defeated. Italy has been taken by the Allies. Ten weeks ago, an invasion force of one hundred and fifty-six thousand British, American and Canadian troops landed in France. The Japanese are also being defeated. All across the Pacific, the American forces are pushing them back. Island by island. It won't be long before we have them on the run.'

'How long?' Nicholas asked.

'Who can tell?' the major answered. 'A matter of months, I'd say. A year. Not longer.'

'Can I ask you a question?' Nicholas requested.

'Fire away!' Major Fox said.

Nicholas hesitated. He wanted to ask a question but he was afraid, terribly afraid, of the answer. He looked along the terrace as if searching for a way to escape from the truth should it not be what he wanted.

It looked so homely. Dai Kam lay in his usual place in front of the temple door. From under the lintel a faint drift of blue smoke rose into the air to be snatched away by a light breeze. On the roof of the gatehouse, Laan Doh Mao slept on the hot tiles. From inside the house,

Nicholas could hear Venerable Grandmother humming and, down the far end of the terrace, a pig squealed.

'What happened to my parents?' Nicholas asked.

'I don't know,' Major Fox said. 'That's the truth. You're not a little boy now, you're almost a man, and I'm not going to lie to you. If your parents were dead, I would tell you. But I really don't know.'

Nicholas left the table and went along the terrace. Hearing his footsteps, Dai Kam half woke, peered at him in a sleep-bleary way then, satisfied it was only Nicholas coming towards him, let his head flop back on the flagstones. Nicholas knelt next to the dog and stroked his side, feeling his ribs moving slowly up and down as he breathed. There was, he thought, still a chance his parents were alive and, as Dai Kam lazily wagged his tail on the stones, Nicholas suddenly recalled one of his mother's favourite expressions – no news is good news.

After a few minutes, Nicholas returned to the table under the tree and said, 'Why have you come here?'

Major Fox looked Nicholas straight in the eye and replied, 'I'll be quite blunt. I need your help to play some music on the bamboo radio.'

He reached under his chair and removed a package the size of a large book from the satchel. It was tied about with string and wrapped in the same kind of dark brown, waterproof paper as had enclosed the explosive.

'I want you to deliver this for me. In Kowloon.'

'Is it a bomb?' Nicholas wanted to know.

'Take it,' Major Fox held the package out. 'But be careful.'

Nicholas accepted the package. His hands dropped as he took it: it weighed far more than he had expected.

'What is it?' Nicholas asked, placing it on the table. 'It's very heavy.'

'Open it,' the major ordered.

Undoing the string, Nicholas folded back the paper to display a small cardboard box. He removed the lid. Inside was a thin envelope, an oblong wrapped in khaki cloth and a glass bottle of cloudy liquid padded round with cotton wool.

'The envelope is a message,' Major Fox said. 'The cloth – well, you unwrap it.'

Nicholas doubled back the material. In it was something which glittered in the dappled sunlight cutting through the tree above.

'That's a bar of gold,' the major said. 'Twelve ounces of twenty-four-carat gold.'

Nicholas ran his finger over it. The surface was smooth and warm.

'How much is it worth?'

'Thousands of dollars,' Major Fox replied, 'but that,' he pointed to the bottle, 'is much more valuable. That's worth hundreds of lives. Human lives.'

'I don't see,' Nicholas said, 'how a small bottle can be worth . . .'

'I'll explain,' interrupted the major. 'In the prison camps in Kowloon, men – British soldiers, sailors and airmen – are dying of a disease called diphtheria. It starts off as nothing more than a sore throat but, within hours, it gets worse and your throat fills with a grey mucus, a sort of sticky film. In less than a day, unless you're very lucky, you're dead. That bottle contains diphtheria prophylactic vaccine, enough to halt the epidemic.'

'And the gold?' Nicholas enquired.

'In time of war,' Major Fox answered cryptically, 'gold is very useful.'

'Why can't Ah Kwan take the package?' Nicholas asked.

'Japanese know me,' Ah Kwan said. 'If he see me, he kill me.' He shrugged. 'If he kill me, no worry! But if I killed . . .'

'. . . the vaccine won't get through,' the major cut in. 'Will you do it? Kwan will go with you to help you but he cannot – he dare not – go close to the prison camp. If the

98

Japanese caught him they would torture him before killing him. Even someone as strong and staunch as Kwan may talk when the torturer starts his work. I can't risk that. Kwan knows too much.'

'Can't you use someone else?' Nicholas ventured.

'I'm afraid not,' the major answered. 'The Japanese had a big drive against us. Most of our agents – our undercover men – were taken, tortured and executed.'

Nicholas looked at the bottle again. It seemed so innocuous, just a little bottle with a red rubber bung secured with a metal clip.

'Hundreds of lives?' he mused out loud.

'At least three hundred,' Major Fox said.

When he had been considering going with Tai Lo Fu to destroy the Waterloo Road bridge, Nicholas had consulted Tang and Ah Mee – and his photograph. Yet now, it seemed to him, he had no choice. This was not a matter of knocking out the Kowloon to Canton railway. This concerned the lives of prisoners. He thought for a moment of his father. If he were alive – and the major had not reported him dead – he might be in that prison camp. It stood to reason. His father had been a soldier, albeit a volunteer one. And he might, at that very moment, be lying on a bed in a fever, his throat sore and getting worse.

'Yes,' Nicholas said at last, his voice quiet and resolute. 'I'll deliver it.'

*

Nicholas lay on the gravelly soil, squirming his way beneath the lantana thicket, pulling himself along on his elbows. The branches snagged his clothing and hat. Every time he crushed a leaf or brushed a floret of blossoms, they gave off the unpleasant smell of cats. The only good thing about the plant, he thought, was that the flowers attracted a myriad of butterflies. Huge swallowtails hovered just over his head, landing on the blooms to taste their nectar. Their wings beat as their long tongues, coiled like watch-springs, unfurled and dipped into the flower-heads. Some of the insects were so close to his face Nicholas could feel the draught of their wings fanning his brow.

Reaching the far end of the thicket, Nicholas found himself on a ledge covered by boulders. Ah Kwan crouched behind one of them, wiping his brow.

'*Ho yit*,' he exclaimed in Cantonese, his voice low. 'Very hot.'

'Hot,' Nicholas confirmed as he edged nearer to Ah Kwan.

Below them, not two hundred metres away, were the streets and tenements of the Sham Shui Po area of Kowloon. Beyond the buildings, the sea shone like liquid mercury under the harsh sun. Only the tree-covered hills of Stonecutters' Island two kilometres offshore offered any respite from the sun's glare.

'Can you see the prison?' Ah Kwan asked.

Nicholas studied the space between the tenements and the sea. He knew where to look from the map of Kowloon which Major Fox had shown him when briefing him on his mission.

Where the tenements ended was a barracks containing twelve rows of accommodation huts, assorted storehouses and other low sheds. In the centre was a parade ground and at one end, backing on to the shoreline, stood a substantial four-storey building with a flat roof.

'You ready?' Ah Kwan ventured.

'I'm ready,' Nicholas declared.

He was surprised not to find himself excited. When he had gone with the partisans to sabotage the bridge, he had felt a huge sense of adventure, an electric charge of danger rush through him. Now he was calm, cool, collected. He had a job to do – a vital job. If he failed, there would be no second chance. Not for him nor for any prisoner who contracted diphtheria.

Checking the package was safe under his jacket, Nicholas looked at Ah Kwan and said, 'I go now.'

Ah Kwan touched his shoulder.

'You are a very brave man,' he said. 'It's very dangerous down there. You take care of yourself.'

Nicholas slipped around the boulders, slithered down a slope of loose stones to a narrow path, adjusted his clothes, tightened the knot in the cord of his cane hat, brushed the dust off his trousers and set off downwards.

As he went, Ah Kwan's voice echoed in his mind. *You are a very brave man*, it said. Not *boy. Man.*

When he reached the streets they were not busy. A few people walked in the cover of the arcaded pavements but there were no shops open or hawkers trading. Compared to the pre-war years, Nicholas found himself in a ghost town.

Indeed, he thought as he walked along, the people were not unlike ghosts. They were squinny, emaciated folk who walked lethargically, without any sense of drive or real purpose. He noticed almost everyone had thin wrists and ankles. The skin on their necks was drawn and their cheekbones were prominent. More than a few had sunken eyes and the flesh around them was tinted with grey.

These, Nicholas realized, were the signs of advanced starvation. They brought to his mind the man who had tried to barter his wife to Tang. He wondered how many of the people around him now had sold their children. The thought sent a shiver down his back and made him feel both guilty and conspicuous. He was well fed, fat by comparison to those around him. He would, he considered, be worth selling himself.

As he turned into a wide road which led towards the prison camp, Nicholas saw ahead a small gathering of a dozen or so people clustered around a doorway. He was instantly on his guard. A group of so many might attract the attention of Japanese soldiers yet, as he watched the crowd, three Japanese officers walked by, casting no more than a cursory glance at the congregation.

Curious, Nicholas approached the people. On the pavement before them squatted an old man with a wooden board laid out in front of him upon which were arranged a number of bits of meat attached to lengths of grey string. It was a few seconds before Nicholas realized what he was looking at. The strings were tails. The old man was selling rats and mice for food.

Half a kilometre further along the road, Nicholas turned left down a street leading to the sea front and arrived at the prison camp main entrance. This consisted of a tall gate and a sentry box with a two-storey stone building to the right. Two Japanese guards occupied the sentry box whilst, just inside the gate, several more lingered in the shade of the building. They paid him not the slightest attention as he stood in the arcade of the tenement building across the street.

The camp perimeter consisted of a barbed-wire fence about four metres high. Behind that was a space about three metres across in which, Nicholas noted, there was a trip wire of some sort then, across the space, another barbed-wire fence.

Between two tenements, fifty metres from the gate, he found an alley which Major Fox had recommended as a temporary hide-out and escape route. He entered it and hunched down behind a derelict cart. The hot air of the late afternoon was stifling, the stink of sewage in the alley almost overpowering, yet Nicholas stuck it out. He had his orders.

At six o'clock, the sound of feet marching along the road signified the return of the forced-labour parties.

Nicholas got up, rubbed his legs to get his circulation going and stepped out of the alley.

Along the road marched a bedraggled column of several hundred prisoners of war, accompanied by Japanese soldiers. They were in a sorry state. Gaunt and dressed in not much better than rags, they were coated with dust, their skins tanned and leathery from working long hours under the sub-tropical sun. Some wore tattered hats, either the remains of their military headgear or bamboo coolie hats, but most were bare-headed. A few were barefoot, their feet horny and their toenails like shavings of horse's hoof.

Nicholas went to the edge of the kerb, joining a small number of onlookers, most of them women. He was watching for one man. As he surveyed the approaching prisoners, he could hear Major Fox informing him: 'Your contact is Flight Lieutenant Drake. His nickname's Frank – after Sir Francis Drake – but his real name is Edwin Charles Drake. Quite tall with a moustache. As he passes you, he will give you a signal by making a circle with the index finger and thumb of his left hand. As soon as he does this, another prisoner will cause a diversion. You slip forward and give him the package. That done, leg it down the alley.'

The column drew nearer. Nicholas risked removing his varnished cane hat so that he might see better and be easily recognized by his contact. He knew his clothing and dark hair would pass muster if seen by the guards from a distance. Besides, the guards marched with their rifles over their shoulders: they were not expecting trouble.

Nicholas let his eyes jump from row to row as the men marched by to wheel right into the camp. He could not see a single man with a moustache. It was not until the end of the column reached him that he saw Flight Lieutenant Drake.

His heart sank. The moustachioed man was not marching. He was being half carried and half dragged between two other prisoners. His head lolled from side to side, his feet hardly able to keep in step with his two supporters. There was no way possible for Nicholas to get the package to him.

Nicholas's thoughts were in turmoil. Major Fox's orders had been firm. 'If you don't succeed,' he had said, 'get back to the rendezvous with Kwan. We'll just have to find another way. Don't concern yourself.' Yet Nicholas was concerned. A lot depended on him and he did not want to be a failure. Furthermore, Drake was plainly semi-conscious. He might have caught diphtheria: the contents of the box could save his life.

At the rear of the column, two Japanese guards kept pace about five metres back. They were not looking at the prisoners but talking to each other.

There was nothing for it. Nicholas had to act – and act fast.

Touching the plum-stone carving hanging around his neck for luck, he darted forward and into the centre of the marching column. As he ran forwards, dropping his hat, he realized his clothing was dark coloured: most of the prisoners wore the remnants of khaki uniforms. He would stick out like a telegraph pole in a tennis court.

Yet there was no turning back. The two guards at the rear had ended their conversation. One was looking at the column.

Two ranks in front of him, Nicholas spied his salvation. It was a prisoner who had clearly once been a Royal Navy petty officer. He wore bedraggled navy blue shorts under a once white shirt. A red warrant officer's badge was still clinging to the sleeve. Nicholas squeezed forward to position himself next to the sailor who was carrying a bucket.

'What're you up to, Johnny?' he asked in an exhausted voice as Nicholas fell in beside him.

Nicholas ignored him. The column turned and, in a matter of metres, he was inside the camp.

The prisoners headed towards the parade ground where a number of Japanese officers stood on a dais. One of them clutched a clipboard. It was obvious what was going to happen: there was going to be a count of prisoners. If he was still in the ranks when the tally was made, Nicholas would be discovered.

The column slowed as the first ranks fanned out into lines. Nicholas, deciding to risk all once more, dashed for the cover of one of the barrack huts.

The wooden steps were only three metres away, but it seemed like thirty. As he leapt up them, he prayed the door was unlocked. If it was not, he would be trapped in full view of the guards at the rear of the column who were now marching smartly behind their charges, putting on a show for their superiors.

His hand hit the door, his fingers grasped the handle and turned. It opened inwards. Nicholas fell into the room, pushing the door closed behind him. Panting hard, he took stock of his surroundings.

The barrack hut was suffocatingly hot, the sun cutting shafts of brilliant light through holes in the roof. The windows were shuttered, leaving the interior gloomy and close. Either side of the long building was lined with three tiers of wooden bunks upon which he could see rush mats, small piles of clothing or blankets, a few tin bowls and other oddments of basic personal property. In the centre were three long tables, some chairs and, halfway down, a cast-iron stove with a chimney pipe going up through the roof. The place smelt of stale sweat and the hot tar melting on the roof.

He sat on the edge of one of the bunks and felt under his jacket. The packet had slipped a little lower in his waistband but it was still there.

The door was abruptly flung open, flooding a beam of late, orange sunlight the length of the barrack. Nicholas ducked under the bunk and held his breath.

Slow, measured footsteps advanced along the wooden boards of the floor, every sound redolent with threat. They came nearer and Nicholas could hear the squeak of polished leather, the soft rub of material.

Into view came a pair of legs encased in black boots reaching to the knee. The leather shone like polished ebony. Into the top were pressed crisply laundered khaki trousers. Down the flank of the left leg hung a Japanese officer's sword.

The legs halted, not a metre from Nicholas's face, and stood motionless. Out of sight above him, Nicholas could imagine the man listening, surveying the barrack for something amiss.

In the near stillness, Nicholas's hearing became acute. He could clearly pick out the distant shouting of orders, the shuffle of feet on dusty soil, the revving of a vehicle engine, even the far-off yapping of a dog. Yet, above them all, like a leading instrument in a strange, muted orchestra, he could hear the Japanese officer breathing.

At last, the legs moved and strolled away. Hollow footfalls sounded as the officer descended the steps. Nicholas took a huge breath. Had he been under water, he would have been on the brink of drowning.

No sooner had Nicholas sucked in a lungful of air than another noise came to him. It was a scrabbling, snuffling, huffing sound. Bizarrely, he thought of a miniature steam train. Then something shot under the bunk, collided with him and started to slap his face with what he thought in his panic was a warm, damp rag.

Nicholas was so startled, he let out a yelp which was answered. Under the bunk with him was a Jack Russell terrier, its ribs showing and a patch of mange on its rump.

'What've you unearthed, Sally?' a deep voice demanded.

'Not benighted rats again,' said another.

'All the poor little bleeder gets to eat,' commented a third. 'At least it's better than what we get.'

Now, around the bunk, there was a forest of bare legs, some in boots, some barefoot.

'Chalky! Get a broom 'andle,' suggested a fourth voice. 'We'll break th' little booger's back when it runs.'

The terrier retreated, sat on the floor and looked under the bunk at Nicholas. It wagged its stumpy tail hard against a booted foot.

Gradually, Nicholas hauled himself forward and out from under the bunk. The prisoners ogled.

'Bloody 'ell!' said one.

'Some rat!' exclaimed a bare-chested man with a sallow complexion and prominent ribs.

'We've got us a Chinese nipper,' declared a third man.

'What – you – wantee?' Sally's owner slowly enquired. He was a thickset prisoner with a tattoo of a semi-naked lady just visible through the coating of dust on his forearm.

Nicholas got to his feet, looked around the ragged band in front of him and said, quite clearly but not too loudly, 'I am English. My Chinese name is Wing-ming but my English name is Nicholas. I have brought you some music on my bamboo radio.'

Silence fell. The prisoners gawped at him and each other. Then the tattooed prisoner turned to his comrades.

'Jock! Watch the door! Chalky! Sticko! Windows! Nobby! Get weaving! Find out when the Nips're having their nosh tonight.'

The prisoners were galvanized into action, looking through the shutters of the windows and minding the door which was closed after Nobby had departed.

'Now,' the tattooed prisoner began. 'I'm Colour Sergeant Parker. You sit yourself down and tell all, lad.'

'I am Nicholas Holford. I'm . . .' he paused and realized he was not sure how old he was: birthdays had not been a part of life at Sek Wan. He hazarded a guess. '. . . fourteen and I live in the New Territories with Chinese people. I have a friend,' he was cautious not to name names, 'who works for BAAG. And he has asked me to bring this into the camp.' He tugged the packet from under his belt. 'I was to pass it to Flight Lieutenant Drake as you marched in but I couldn't.'

'Frankie's got the fever,' observed a prisoner.

'Fine,' said Colour Sergeant Parker, 'but how the hell did you get in here?'

Nicholas recounted how he had hidden in the column, slipped through the gate, run for the barrack and how the Japanese officer had come in.

'That was Donkey Face,' Parker remarked. 'Nasty piece of work. We wondered what he was after. Must have seen the door go.'

Nobby returned and said tersely, 'Twenty hundred hours.'

Parker nodded and said to Nicholas, 'Right! At eight o'clock, there'll be fewer Japs wandering about. They'll be busying chowing down to their suppers. That's when we'll get you over to Jubilee Buildings, the big billet on the waterfront. You can hand your package over, then we'll get you out of the camp.'

For an hour and a half, as night came on, Nicholas remained in the barrack. The prisoners' food detail arrived. He was appalled to see that all they were given to eat was boiled rice floating in hot water with a few fish heads bobbing on the surface. The prisoners offered him a bowlful but he declined it: partly, he felt guilty at being so well fed himself and partly he could not bear seeing the fish eyes staring at him from the stew-pot.

At the appointed time, Nobby and Parker guided Nicholas through the camp to Jubilee Buildings where he was taken to the second floor and into a small room in which an austere-looking man was seated at a table.

He wore the remains of a battlefield blouse with pips on his shoulders.

'So you're a musician,' the officer greeted Nicholas, standing up and shaking his hand firmly. 'A brave chappie and no mistake.'

'How do you do, sir,' Nicholas replied.

'We've got to get a move on,' the officer went on. 'The Nips'll only be in their mess for at most fifteen minutes. Let's get down to business. What's the music you're playing?'

Nicholas handed over the package and the officer unwrapped it immediately. He tore the envelope open, quickly read the message, removed the block of gold and picked up the bottle, scanning the label.

'You know what this is?' the officer enquired, looking at the two soldiers.

'It's something to stop diphtheria,' Nicholas said, thinking the question was aimed at him.

'Too right, it is,' the officer declared. 'You're more than a little musician, lad. You're a bloody guardian angel. It's a pity we haven't got time to introduce you to our camp medic, Dr Coombes. I'm sure he'd want to thank you personally. You'll have saved a lot of lives with this.'

There was a gentle double knock on the door. A head appeared round it, murmured, 'Nips beginning to come on the move, sir!' then vanished.

'We've got to get you out of here,' the officer announced urgently. 'PDQ. Pretty damn quick! The guards've had their dinner and we've . . .' He glanced at the other prisoners. 'Well, put it this way, not all of us inmates are entirely trustworthy and we don't want the wrong element to hear about your visit. At least, not while you're still here.' He unbuttoned the flap of one of the chest pockets of his blouse. 'Will you take a message back for me? Give it to whoever sent you, or to someone you can trust implicitly to pass it on down the line. This has to get through to Chungking.' At that, the officer handed Nicholas a length of bamboo about the size of a fountain pen. The hollow ends were sealed with candle wax. 'Don't lose it,' he went on, 'but, if you get in a tight spot, drop it. If possible, burn it.'

The door opened again and the head appeared briefly once more to mutter, 'Nips away, sir!'

'Time to go,' declared Colour Sergeant Parker.

The officer shook Nicholas's hand again. 'I pray we meet after the war, son,' he said gravely. 'I won't forget your courage.'

'I hope you can swim,' Parker said as he and Nobby hurried Nicholas along a corridor and out on to a veranda which ran the length of the building, 'because the only way out is with the fishes.'

Halfway along the veranda, a rope had been tied around a pillar and thrown out over the barbed-wire fence to dangle into the sea.

'You've got to be snappy,' the Colour Sergeant warned, pointing along the sea wall. 'Take a decko at that.' Nicholas glanced to his right. Two hundred metres away was a tall watch-tower. 'In a few minutes, that'll have a couple of eagle-eyed bastards back up it with a searchlight so bright you could spot it from the moon.'

Nicholas looked down at the black sea below. He could hear the waves lapping the sea wall.

'When you reach the water,' Nobby told him, 'head away from the tower. Keep close to the wall until you come to the second set of steps. You'll be safe then.'

'Can't you escape this way?' Nicholas asked.

'No chance,' Nobby replied, helping him on to the parapet of the veranda. 'We're too weak to swim it. Besides, we can't make it into China. The Nips'd hunt us down in no time. Nope, we're stuck here for the duration.' He glanced in the direction of the tower. 'Better get yourself off. Double-quick, lad!'

Nicholas wrapped his legs round the rope and, checking the bamboo message holder was safely in his pocket, started to lower himself. Where the rope reached the perimeter fence, Nicholas had to carefully negotiate the roll of tangled barbed concertina wire on top. He tore his trousers and gashed his arm but he made it to the sea. The salt water made the cut sting.

Swimming as close to the sea wall as he could, Nicholas reached the steps and cautiously climbed them to discover he was facing the tenement buildings. Getting his bearings, he ran to the alleyway and, after ripping off the torn leg of his trousers to bind round his wound, he headed for the hills. His sopping wet clothing clung to him but in no way dampened his feelings of intense elation.

When he finally clambered up to the boulder-strewn ledge, he found Ah Kwan anxiously waiting for him in the night.

'You've taken longer to come,' Ah Kwan whispered. 'I was thinking bad thoughts.'

'I had to go into the camp,' Nicholas replied.

'You went in!' Ah Kwan retorted incredulously.

Nicholas smiled and, producing the sealed bamboo tube from his pocket, he handed it to Ah Kwan. 'I went in,' he said proudly. 'I played music on the bamboo radio.'

Part Five

1945

Nicholas, standing in the prow of the sampan, leapt on to the quay and ran the mooring rope through an iron ring. Once the craft was secure, he and Tang unloaded their two baskets of dried fish then placed a large wooden tub on the quay which Nicholas filled with sea-water. Tang tipped in that morning's catch and the fish swam frantically round the sides of the tub.

Since he had been helping Tang with the fishing, Nicholas had learnt a lot more than how to repair nets. He could bait lines, fish on a moonless night with a lantern to attract the catch, set crab baskets, tell where prawns could be found and understand why Tang sold his fish alive in tubs – no Chinese would consider his food fresh unless he saw it moving.

Within minutes of setting out their catch, people came to buy. Some customers offered Japanese five-yen notes, over-printed in red to denote occupation currency: Tang accepted them with reluctance. A few proffered old-fashioned silver dollars or Imperial cash with square holes in the middle of the coins. Most bartered, the haggling intense with each party determined to get the best bargain possible. Tang never refused an item: a square of fraying silk, a tatty garment, a piece of jade, a chipped rice bowl, a tiny fragment of gold, a pair of blunt scissors, a bundle of firewood – whatever it was it ended up in the sampan. On the way back to Sek Wan, Tang would throw the useless or broken items overboard. The first time Nicholas saw him do this, he was amazed.

'That means you've just given the fish away!' he exclaimed as a cracked teapot hit the surface and sank.

'Yes,' said Tang, 'but the people want eat. If I give fish, they feel shame because they poor. So I let them buy. But,' he held up a broken tin-plated alarm clock, 'why I want clock no work?' and he tossed it into the sea.

When the fish were sold, Nicholas and Tang set off through the village towards the tea-house. In the main street, they came upon a large crowd of chattering, laughing people. It was so unusual to see not only a large gathering but also a jolly one that Tang and Nicholas, who would normally have avoided such a throng, joined it to see the cause of the merriment.

Working their way to the front, they came upon an itinerant showman squatting on the ground with a rosewood xylophone. He was in a mid-flow, talking fast, his voice rising and falling, the people laughing and chortling at his words. Next to him was a wooden box with holes drilled in it.

'What's he saying?' Nicholas whispered to Tang. 'I can't understand him.'

'He travelling story-teller, come from north China, talk different accent from Cantonese, not all same like Hong Kong people.'

'But what's he saying?' Nicholas reiterated.

'He tell funny story,' Tang said, his face split with a smile at the latest joke.

'What about?'

'I no can say in English,' Tang replied.

Nicholas, the humour lost on him, was all for leaving. He was not only unable to share in the laughter but he was also thirsty and looking forward to his bowl of tea.

'No go yet,' Tang said. 'Two minute, you laugh.'

The showman picked up two little round-headed hammers with flexible bamboo handles and started to play the xylophone, striking the keys rapidly yet lightly. A delicate tune rose from the instrument, wafting into the air. It was wistful yet strident, a strange kind of music such as Nicholas had never heard before. When the tune ended, the crowd applauded and the showman, after a few more quick and obviously funny words – for the crowd were in stitches – opened the box next to him.

Out jumped a small grey monkey dressed in a miniature Japanese officer's khaki uniform with a forage cap on his head and a little cross strap and belt from which hung a tiny sword. He also held a little carved wooden rifle and bayonet, with the blade painted silver.

The crowd hooted and howled with laughter. Nicholas joined in. He got the joke this time.

The showman played a little tune to which the monkey danced a clumsy jig, swinging his rifle in the air. The moment the music stopped, the monkey stood to attention, the rifle against his shoulder, but upside down. At this, the crowd positively exploded with mirth.

Holding up his little hammers, the showman said something and the crowd fell silent. He then brought the hammers down lightly upon the keys and, to Nicholas's amazement, played 'Rule Britannia!'. The monkey remained at attention until the fourth bar of the tune when he slowly and solemnly set off marching forwards, the inverted rifle at the slope.

The crowd was beside itself with laughter. Nicholas's ribs ached. Tang was red in the face and gasping for his breath. A woman standing next to him had tears of merriment running down her cheeks.

The music stopped. The monkey stood to attention. The showman rattled the hammers against the frame of the xylophone in mimicry of a machine-gun. The monkey dropped its toy gun, staggered forwards, clutching its chest and squeaking in a high-pitched voice. When it

114

reached the xylophone, it looked up at the crowd with piteous eyes and rolled over, feigning dead.

Everyone applauded and laughed uproariously. Several people stepped forwards and dropped a coin on the monkey's box. Someone gave him half of one of Nicholas's dried fish in lieu of payment. The showman stood up and bowed. The monkey revived and also bowed, the forage cap falling off its head.

'Very funny monkey!' Tang exclaimed as the crowd dispersed. 'All same like Japanese . . .'

His words faded. The people around had fallen silent, too.

From the direction of the mountains came a steady, distant drone of aircraft engines. The people who, only a few minutes earlier, had been laughing fit to burst were now serious-faced, looking about for places in which to take cover.

'Run sampan!' Tang shouted to Nicholas in English, abandoning all sense of propriety.

They turned and sprinted for the quayside. In the boat, close against the dock wall, they would be comparatively safe.

They were too late. The aircraft sound swelled to an air-shivering crescendo and burst forth about them. Nicholas glanced upwards as he ran, to see if he could judge where the bombs might fall.

Yet no bombs dropped. Instead, a blizzard of sheets of paper fluttered down on the houses. Through it, Nicholas could see the marking on the aircraft's wings. It was a white bar through a blue circle containing a white five-pointed star.

A man ran by, shouting, '*Mei gwok! Mei gwok!*'

Tang stopped running.

'What does it mean?' Nicholas asked. 'What does *mei gwok* mean?'

Tang smiled and said, '*Mei gwok* mean America.'

Reaching up, he caught one of the sheets of paper which were drifting down all round them. Upon it was printed a message in Chinese.

'What does it say?' Nicholas asked impatiently.

'It say,' Tang replied, 'Japanese no win war.'

*

Six weeks later, Tang returned early from a day's fishing. Nicholas was sweeping out the pigsties when the sampan hove into view. Tang was rowing so hard the whole vessel violently pitched and yawed. He was still a hundred metres from the shingle beach when he started shouting.

Nicholas and the others rushed down to the shore. Tang did not even bother to run the sampan aground. He leapt from it into the shallows, shouting, '*Lai! Lai!* Come! Come! *Fai! Fai!* Quick! Quick!' and set off towards the promontory.

The others followed. Even Venerable Grandmother and Grandfather came, hobbling as fast as they could.

Brushing through the scrub, they reached the family grave to find Tang staring out to sea, shading his face with his hands. They gathered around him.

'Look!' Tang said. 'You see?'

Nicholas screwed his eyes half closed against the glare of the sun on the sea. Far out, beyond the islands, he could just make out a low grey shape near the horizon.

'What is it?' he asked.

Tang put his arm around Ah Mee and said, 'British navy ship.'

The next morning, as soon as it was light, Nicholas and Tang set off for Sai Kung. They arrived to find the little harbour packed with sampans and junks, and the village in festive uproar. Several houses were hung with red lanterns, the tea-house was packed and a huge crowd was gathered before the temple. Tang purchased a packet of joss-sticks and joined the mass of people shuffling forward to light the incense and place it in a brass urn before the effigy.

'Tang,' Nicholas asked, 'will you give me a few joss-sticks?'

For a minute Tang looked at Nicholas, then he handed him half the packet. When he had nearly reached the front of the crowd, Nicholas lit his joss-sticks from an oil lamp, moved forward, held the sticks between his hands, placed together as if in prayer, bowed three times and stuck the incense in the sand in the urn.

As he stepped away from the effigy, he felt a great sense of peace come over him. The war was over. He had survived. The Tangs and Qing-mai had survived. And yet, as he felt the relief sweep over him so he experienced a fear. What would the future hold?

That evening, Venerable Grandmother roasted one of the latest litter of piglets and Venerable Grandfather produced a bottle of rice wine he had been hoarding away to celebrate the end of the war. After the meal was over, as Nicholas sat alone with his thoughts on the terrace in the twilight, Qing-mai came and sat next to him, placing a small package on the terrace wall.

'Tomorrow,' she said, 'you are going back to Hong Kong island with Tang and Ah Mee.'

Nicholas did not reply. He looked down at the beach and the sampan wallowing near the mouth of the Dragon Tail Stream.

'Are you not happy?' Qing-mai asked.

'I don't know,' Nicholas answered. 'I don't know what will happen. My life . . . Sek Wan is my life. You are all my life. I don't . . . I don't really remember what it was like . . . before . . . What it was like to live with my parents.' He paused. Dai Kam ambled by and he reached down, letting his fingers stroke the dog as it passed. 'I don't even know if I have any parents.'

'If not,' Qing-mai said quietly, putting her hand on Nicholas's, 'then Tang and Ah Mee must be your parents now. And I will be like your sister. Venerable Grandfather . . .'

'I don't want to leave,' Nicholas declared. 'This is my home now.'

'But you must go,' Qing-mai replied. 'And you can always come back. It is not so far.'

'What are you going to do?' Nicholas asked.

'I will stay here. Wait for my father to come.'

In front of the terrace, there was a brief rustling sound in the air. A bat flickered across the space of sky in front of the lychee tree.

'In China,' Qing-mai said, 'if a bat flies over people, they will be very lucky.' She passed the package along the wall to Nicholas. 'This is for you,' she said. 'My present for you to take.'

'What is it?' Nicholas enquired.

'My poem.'

'Your poem?' Nicholas answered.

'My poem,' Qing-mai repeated. 'The poem of my life.'

She leaned across then and kissed Nicholas on his cheek. He could feel her eyelashes tickle his skin. Her face was wet and he turned to realize she had been crying.

*

The ferries were not yet operating so Tang had to hire a sampan to take them across the harbour from Kowloon to the island of Hong Kong. As the boatman propelled the sampan over the choppy waves, Nicholas counted two aircraft carriers, a battleship and several smaller fighting vessels, a merchant cruiser and a hospital ship all riding at anchor or moored alongside the docks. At the bow of every vessel flew the white ensign of the Royal Navy.

Landing at a jetty on the island, Nicholas and the Tangs had to stand aside as a column of dejected Japanese troops was marched by, surrounded by a contingent of Royal Marines with fixed bayonets. Along the pavement, Chinese stood three deep, cheering.

When the column had passed, they set off up the steep streets in the direction of Peony Villa. At every corner, people talked animatedly. Windows were open with laundry hanging out on poles to dry. In Hollywood Road, a long queue had formed outside a rice shop which was being guarded by three Marines and a Royal Naval officer.

As they walked, Nicholas recognized nothing until they reached the street where, it seemed a lifetime ago, he had seen the two Japanese soldiers. Under the bauhinia tree seated at a very rickety table, two old men were sitting chattering away like sparrows. In the branches above them, a golden finch chirped in a cage. Near by, the barber had set up a stool and was waiting for a customer.

An hibiscus hedge lined the road, unkempt and badly in need of pruning. Through the branches, Nicholas could just make out iron railings and a gate leaning on its hinges. Glancing up, between the sheer mountain behind and the tops of trees, he could see a tiled roof.

'There you house,' Ah Mee said.

Tang opened the gate. It squeaked rustily. The path beyond was strewn with dead leaves. Weeds poked up through the gravel.

Looking up, Nicholas found he could not remember the house. Not exactly. He could recall Victoria Peak rising behind it but not the actual building itself although certain aspects of it stirred a memory. The shutters seemed somehow familiar, the veranda and the palm tree by the front door.

At the foot of the lawn, they halted. The house stood before them. The window-sills were peeling. Several shutters were missing, showing jagged broken glass in the frames. There were dark holes in the roof where there should have been tiles. On the veranda, one of the plant pots remained but it was cracked open. The earth had spilled out and was growing weeds.

Nicholas did not want to go on. He could not account for it, but he was afraid, as scared as he had been nearly four years before when Ah Kwan had grabbed him from behind.

Tang, who had gone ahead, beckoned to him.

'We go in,' he said.

The front door was ajar, the lock smashed, the brass handle and letter-box stolen. Nicholas slowly pushed it open. The interior of the building was cool and dark. He entered the hallway. It was bare of furniture and the wallpaper was torn and curling off the walls. Some floorboards had been removed leaving gaping holes. He pushed at the door into the drawing room. Like the hallway, the room had been stripped of furniture. Not even the light switches by the door remained, just bare wires protruding from the plaster. The room smelt mouldy.

Careful to avoid more holes in the floor, Nicholas stepped towards the window. The frame was missing and the shutters were awry. He pushed the shutters out and sunlight flooded into the room.

A faint noise behind him made him turn. Standing in the doorway was a European woman wearing a faded floral print dress. Her blonde hair was untidy and she wore no make-up. Upon her feet, Nicholas noticed, she had a pair of army boots.

For a moment, they stared at each other then she said, in not much more than a whisper, 'Nicky.'

Nicholas made no move. He just looked at the woman. Her face was drawn and her wrists were so thin that, in the bright sunlight, Nicholas could see the blue veins criss-crossing beneath her skin. Around her eyes was a light grey shadow. In contrast, her lips were almost colourless.

'Nicky?' she ventured again.

Was this woman his mother? She did not look like the woman in the photograph. That woman was young and vibrant: the one standing before him looked old and exhausted. What was more, he was taller than she was: his mother, he remembered, was at least head and shoulders taller than him.

'I am Wing-mi . . .' Nicholas began then, pausing, gathered himself up and continued, 'I am Nicholas Holford.'

The woman slowly stepped forward. Her arms were outstretched. Her heavy boots clomped on the bare boards.

'Oh, Nicky . . .' she said, her eyes filling with tears.

Over the woman's shoulder, Nicholas caught sight of Tang and Ah Mee standing in the doorway. They were holding hands and looked, he thought, so much younger than they really were, and happy, like people in love for the first time.

The woman reached the middle of the room. Nicholas gazed into her face.

'Watch out for the floor, Mum,' he said. 'Some of the boards are missing.'

Heinemann
New Windmills

Founding Editors: Anne and Ian Serraillier

Chinua Achebe Things Fall Apart
David Almond Skellig
Maya Angelou I Know Why the Caged Bird Sings
Margaret Atwood The Handmaid's Tale
Jane Austen Pride and Prejudice
J G Ballard Empire of the Sun
Stan Barstow Joby; A Kind of Loving
Nina Bawden Carrie's War; Devil by the Sea; Kept in the Dark; The
Finding; Humbug
Lesley Beake A Cageful of Butterflies
Malorie Blackman Tell Me No Lies; Words Last Forever
Martin Booth Music on the Bamboo Radio
Ray Bradbury The Golden Apples of the Sun; The Illustrated Man
Betsy Byars The Midnight Fox; The Pinballs; The Not-Just-Anybody
Family; The Eighteenth Emergency
Victor Canning The Runaways
Jane Leslie Conly Racso and the Rats of NIMH
Robert Cormier We All Fall Down
Roald Dahl Danny, The Champion of the World; The Wonderful
Story of Henry Sugar; George's Marvellous Medicine; The BFG;
The Witches; Boy; Going Solo; Matilda; My Year
Anita Desai The Village by the Sea
Charles Dickens A Christmas Carol; Great Expectations;
Hard Times; Oliver Twist; A Charles Dickens Selection
Peter Dickinson Merlin Dreams
Berlie Doherty Granny was a Buffer Girl; Street Child
Roddy Doyle Paddy Clarke Ha Ha Ha
Anne Fine The Granny Project
Jamila Gavin The Wheel of Surya
Graham Greene The Third Man and The Fallen Idol; Brighton Rock
Thomas Hardy The Withered Arm and Other Wessex Tales
L P Hartley The Go-Between
Ernest Hemmingway The Old Man and the Sea; A Farewell to Arms
Frances Mary Hendry Chandra
Barry Hines A Kestrel For A Knave
Nigel Hinton Getting Free; Buddy; Buddy's Song; Out of the
Darkness
Anne Holm I Am David

Janni Howker Badger on the Barge; The Nature of the Beast; Martin Farrell
Pete Johnson The Protectors
Jennifer Johnston Shadows on Our Skin
Geraldine Kaye Comfort Herself
Daniel Keyes Flowers for Algernon
Clive King Me and My Million
Dick King-Smith The Sheep-Pig
Elizabeth Laird Red Sky in the Morning; Kiss the Dust
D H Lawrence The Fox and The Virgin and the Gypsy; Selected Tales
George Layton The Swap
Harper Lee To Kill a Mockingbird
Julius Lester Basketball Game
C Day Lewis The Otterbury Incident
Joan Lingard Across the Barricades; The File on Fraulein Berg
Penelope Lively The Ghost of Thomas Kempe
Jack London The Call of the Wild; White Fang
Bernard MacLaverty Cal; The Best of Bernard Mac Laverty
Margaret Mahy The Haunting
Anthony Masters Wicked
James Vance Marshall Walkabout
Ian McEwan The Daydreamer; A Child in Time
Pat Moon The Spying Game
Michael Morpurgo My Friend Walter; The Wreck of the Zanzibar; The War of Jenkins' Ear; Why the Whales Came; Arthur, High King of Britain
Beverley Naidoo No Turning Back
Bill Naughton The Goalkeeper's Revenge
New Windmill A Charles Dickens Selection
New Windmill Book of Classic Short Stories
New Windmill Book of Fiction and Non-fiction: Taking Off!
New Windmill Book of Haunting Tales
New Windmill Book of Humorous Stories: Don't Make Me Laugh
New Windmill Book of Nineteenth Century Short Stories
New Windmill Book of Non-fiction: Get Real!
New Windmill Book of Non-fiction: Real Lives, Real Times
New Windmill Book of Scottish Short Stories
New Windmill Book of Short Stories: Fast and Curious
New Windmill Book of Short Stories: Tales with a Twist

How many have you read?